A FR[...]

Annabel Fidelity Bunce – dreamer, champion of justice, seeker after truth, renowned for her high ideals and low cunning! No wonder her life is full of ups and downs and she finds herself in the most extraordinary and hilarious situations.

In these five stories, thirteen-year-old Annabel, with her best friend Kate patiently and admiringly in tow, becomes Mum to a duckling, turns detective to solve the mystery of the *Satyr Tragopan* set free from the tropical bird park, searches for a boy to invite to the Third Year disco, campaigns for the Mill Lane gang's right to play on the green and reveals to Miles Noggins the tragic story behind her middle name.

Whether she's negotiating with Mrs Stringer, fat busybody and prominent member of the Town Council, buttering up Mrs da Susa, the Deputy Head, or pining after local boy turned pop-star Barrie Prince, Annabel's escapades will win her many friends. And Alan Davidson's wickedly observant story-telling will win him many fans.

A Friend Like Annabel is the first of Alan Davidson's books about the irrepressible Annabel, which include *Just Like Annabel*, also published in Puffin. He is also the author of the marvellously gripping story *The Bewitching of Alison Allbright*. He is married, has four children and lives in Dorset.

Another book by Alan Davidson

JUST LIKE ANNABEL

ALAN DAVIDSON

*****

A friend like Annabel

PUFFIN BOOKS

PUFFIN BOOKS

Published by the Penguin Group
27 Wrights Lane, London W8 5TZ, England
Viking Penguin Inc., 40 West 23rd Street, New York, New York 10010, USA
Penguin Books Australia Ltd, Ringwood, Victoria, Australia
Penguin Books Canada Ltd, 2801 John Street, Markham, Ontario, Canada L3R 1B4
Penguin Books (NZ) Ltd, 182–190 Wairau Road, Auckland 10, New Zealand

Penguin Books Ltd, Registered Offices: Harmondsworth, Middlesex, England

First published by Granada Publishing 1983
Published by Viking Kestrel 1988
Published in Puffin Books 1989
1 3 5 7 9 10 8 6 4 2

Reproduced, printed and bound in Great Britain by
Hazell Watson & Viney Limited
Member of BPCC plc
Aylesbury, Bucks, England
Set in Trump Mediaeval

Contents

*****

For Tessa

Annabel
and the duckling

*****

'I saw your friend Annabel in the High Street while I was out,' said Kate's mother over tea. 'There was a duck following her around. It went into the newsagent's after her.'

'Yes,' said Kate, absently.

There was a silence during which Kate went on munching reflectively. Her brother Robert continued to read a comic under the table. He wasn't supposed to do this at meals but since Mr Stocks was himself immersed in a newspaper Robert knew he could get away with it.

'Well!' said Mrs Stocks crossly. 'I know I'm usually supposed to talk to myself at meal-times but I should have thought that what I've just said was worth a comment from *somebody*.'

'Oh, mum,' said Robert, turning over a page, 'that's old news, that's dullsville. Everybody in Addendon knows that Annabel Bunce has got a duck following her around. Why's your news always so stale?'

'*Sorry*,' said Mrs Stocks.

'Anyway, mum,' said Kate, 'it does upset me the way you always say *your friend* Annabel as if *you* don't even know her. It's as if you're getting at her.'

1

'Of course I'm not getting at her. It's just that . . . that . . .'

'Just that *your friend* Annabel is off her head and best kept at a distance,' muttered Robert.

Annabel Fidelity Bunce was Kate's best friend. They lived quite near each other in Addendon, Kate in Oakwood Crescent and Annabel in Badger's Close. They were both in the Third Year at Lord Willoughby's Comprehensive School.

Kate was devoted to Annabel. Mr Toogood, their English teacher, had once asked the class to write a homework essay entitled *My best friend*, without naming the friend of course. Kate had waxed lyrical.

'I think of X as my *smouldering* friend,' she had written. 'She is often tempestuous but can be calm and saintly, too. She feels things very deeply, whether it be elation or anger or despair or whatever. She will be very beautiful when she grows up. She's rather spotty at present but then aren't we all or a lot of us anyway and when that goes she'll be stunning to look at, especially if she can stop slouching as well. I'm very proud to be her best friend and I hope I always shall be. She has a brilliant mind.'

It had caused Mr Toogood, who could easily guess the subject of the essay, to raise his eyebrows. Looking at it some time afterwards, Kate thought that perhaps it was immature but contained much truth. Annabel herself, who had nosily poked through Kate's schoolbag until she found it, thought it masterly, with only minor reservations. She had refused to let Kate see *her* essay.

'But why did Annabel have a duck following her?' persisted Mrs Stocks.

'Oh, the duck – that's Dalton.'

'He's her son,' added Robert, 'or, looked at another way, she's his mother.'

Mr Stocks folded up his newspaper and laid it down beside his plate.

'Put that comic away, Robert,' he said sternly. 'How many times do I have to tell you about reading at the table?'

'His mother?' repeated Mrs Stocks.

'Yes,' said Kate. 'Didn't I tell you? I was there at the birth.'

Annabel Bunce had become a duck's mother. It was careless of her because it was only recently that Miss Ballantyne, their biology teacher at Lord Willoughby's, had been talking in the classroom about ducklings and their odd habits.

Miss Ballantyne was young and pretty and the Third Year – Annabel and Kate were in 3G – were quite fond of her. She had been going out for some time with Mr Rogers, who, apart from teaching maths, also took the boys for some football. It was rumoured, however, that Miss Ballantyne was double-crossing him with Mr Polegate, the Director of Music, a more sensitive and artistic person than Mr Rogers and perhaps more suitable for her. She had twice been seen in his company after school and there was much eager speculation as to whether the two masters would soon be fighting over her and, if so, what Mr Rogers would do to Mr Polegate.

'It may be that you already know,' Miss Ballantyne had told the class in her much-imitated breathless voice, 'that when a duckling comes out of its shell it attaches itself to the first living thing that it sees in the belief that it's found its mother.'

No, Annabel hadn't known that and it was the sort of frivolous titbit of information that appealed to her and came as welcome relief after all the complicated talk recently about photosynthesis and leaf structure. She ceased gazing dreamily out of the window at the spring sunshine and paid attention.

'Of course,' breathed Miss Ballantyne, 'normally the first thing a duckling sees *is* its mother. But not always. There have been cases where ducklings have attached themselves to animals or even to human beings and insisted on following them around. It's got a name. It's called imprinting.'

'Imagine!' Annabel murmured to Kate, who sat next to her. 'Fascinating, isn't it?'

It was on the following Sunday afternoon that Annabel fell into Addendon pond. She and Kate had been idly throwing pieces of bread to a group of rather stand-offish ducks and their ducklings which were drifting about. As a result of an over-enthusiastic throw, her plastic bangle came off her wrist and sailed into the water too and it was whilst reaching down the bank, which is steep at that point, that she slipped and fell in amongst the reeds, sitting down in the water with an enormous splash.

Annabel was furious and so were the ducks and ducklings. Numbers of them came scurrying out of the reeds and made for the opposite side of the pond, casting little glances of distaste at her out of the corners of their eyes.

Annabel rose to her feet, dripping and slimy. Addendon pond is a big one, in the old part of the town by the church. It's full of pondweed and reeds and tadpoles. Moorhens croak in the more inaccessible parts. It's also muddy and a little smelly so Annabel was muddy and a little smelly too as, having scooped up her bangle, she plodded out of the pond bad-temperedly kicking aside the vegetation.

Then suddenly she gave a piercing cry.

'Oh, Kate!' she wailed. 'Come and look what I've done. I've trodden on a duck's nest and there's a duckling just out of its shell.'

Kate hurried over. On the ground amongst the reeds by the edge of the pond lay the remains of the nest which Annabel had trodden on and four broken egg shells. Standing weakly by them and looking plaintively up at Annabel was a tiny duckling. It had a perplexed and helpless look about it that plainly tore at Annabel's heart.

'Hardly out of his dear little shell and he gets his home kicked to pieces by a brute like me!' cried Annabel, picking up the downy little bundle and pressing it dramatically to her cheek.

'It looks as if he was the last of the brood,' said Kate, turning over the empty egg shells with the toe of her shoe. 'His brothers and sisters must be out on the pond. They fled when you fell in, I expect.'

'The baby of the family,' said Annabel, fondly.

Kate suddenly remembered something.

'Annabel, hadn't you better be careful? Remember what Miss Ballantyne said. You may be giving him ideas.'

Annabel blenched. 'You're right, Kate. I was forgetting that. He might get imprinted. He might think I'm his mother.'

She put him down. He looked forlorn.

'Sorry about that,' said Annabel, backing away. 'You do understand, don't you? I'd be a rotten mother. It wouldn't be fair on you.'

He continued to look at her appealingly.

'It wouldn't work,' said Annabel, desperately continuing to back away. 'Honestly, it wouldn't.'

The duckling girded itself, then tottered after her.

'I think it's too late, Annabel,' said Kate. 'I think

he's made up his mind who you are. You now have a son. Or maybe it's a daughter.'

'Well, what could I do?' Annabel asked Miss Ballantyne at school next morning. 'I couldn't just leave him there an *orphan*, could I?'

'No, I suppose not,' breathed Miss Ballantyne, perplexed.

She was gazing rather helplessly at Dalton, as Annabel had called the duckling, after Mr Dalton their chemistry teacher, whose walk had similar characteristics.

Annabel was standing in front of the class, by Miss Ballantyne's desk, with Dalton in a basket. He nestled there happily, giving fat, contented cheeps, obviously well pleased with the family he thought he'd been born into.

Annabel's parents, who had learned tolerance over the years, hadn't minded her arriving home with Dalton, although her father had made some boring jokes about Christmas dinner which she had ignored. But they had flatly refused to let him stay in the house, much though he would have liked to have remained with Annabel the whole time. Mr Bunce had brought out the old rabbit hutch and taken the legs off it so Dalton could sleep in it and he had advised Annabel to start him off with some mash and a saucer of water to drink from, though not to bathe in.

Mr Bunce knew about ducks.

'When he gets bigger you can give him some boiled potatoes and he can peck around the lawn,' he'd said. 'That is, if he's still going to be here when he gets bigger.'

'I hope he isn't,' said Annabel's mother. 'This isn't any place for a duck. He ought to be on the pond with the others.'

6

'It's quite all right, mum,' Annabel had assured her. 'I don't *want* to keep him here any longer than I have to. It's just for a day or two, that's all. The last thing I want is to have a duck following me around all the time. The very last thing.'

'You are sure you wouldn't like to keep the – the relationship?' said Miss Ballantyne now.

'Positive,' said Annabel.

'Because it's most interesting really and it could be very instructive for the whole class. I've only read about these cases before and now we all have a chance to study imprinting in action.'

She looked at Annabel quite hopefully.

'Not for long,' said Annabel firmly. She picked Dalton up and put him down on the floor, from where he looked up at her raptly. When she took a pace backwards, he moved after her.

'You see? He's very sweet but I wouldn't have a life of my own, would I? Anyway, it's not fair on him.'

'Oh, well,' sighed Miss Ballantyne, 'I suppose we could at least try introducing him to his real mother. That would be an interesting experiment in itself.' She looked at her watch. 'We've just about got time to spend the lesson by the pond today. We'll get some stale bread from the kitchens to take with us.'

Annabel was more than usually popular as the whole class trooped off in a long line to watch the reunion.

The ducks were, as usual, out on the pond in force. The trouble was, of course, that no one knew which of them *was* Dalton's real mother.

'I think that perhaps the best thing,' said Miss Ballantyne, 'would be to hold a sort of identification parade. Annabel, if you were to put Dalton where the ducks could see him and we were then to attract them near him with bread, it may be that some sort of

7

reaction will take place. Either Dalton might instinctively feel drawn to one of the ducks or a duck might feel protective towards Dalton and take him under her wing.'

While Kate and the rest of the class threw bits of bread, Annabel carefully placed Dalton by the edge of the pond. Some of the boys were placing bets as to which duck, if any, would claim him.

He looked rather bored as the ducks came sailing in to pick up the bread, gazing at them without interest. However, to the considerable excitement of the class and particularly of Richard White, who'd backed it, one duck with three ducklings in tow heaved itself out of the water, apparently with the intention of inspecting Dalton more closely.

Annabel gripped Kate's arm tensely. 'Note,' she hissed, 'three ducklings. That's the size of Dalton's family.'

The duck scratched itself heavily and contemplated Dalton enigmatically. Dalton looked studiously away and then, nervous of the duck's intentions, made for the safety of Annabel.

The duck, meanwhile, turned and went quacking off in the direction of a piece of bread which had fallen amongst the grass, the reason for its getting out of the pond in the first place. The other ducks drifted away again and Richard White's face fell.

'The trouble is,' said Miss Ballantyne, disappointed, 'that Dalton doesn't know he's a duckling. You see, he's never been able to look in a mirror and study himself so he doesn't know *what* he is. By now he probably thinks he looks like us. That is –' her pretty face clouded over for a moment '– if he thinks anything at all.'

'I think he thinks ducks are silly things,' said Annabel, who was even more disappointed than Miss

Ballantyne. 'He just doesn't have anything in common with them any more.'

Dalton gave her a devoted look.

'At any rate,' said Kate, 'it looks as if you're stuck with him.'

Annabel picked him up and put him back in his basket. She looked very disconsolate.

'I think,' said Miss Ballantyne, 'that I'd better give you some instructions on how to look after him, for the time being, anyway. You'll have to feed him properly, of course, but I think you'll find the most demanding part is the swimming lessons.'

'Swimming lessons?' said Annabel. 'I *can* swim.'

'But he can't,' explained Miss Ballantyne, 'and if you're going to be his mother you'll have to teach him. It simply means giving him a lead, that's all. You swim and he'll follow. But make sure his back doesn't get wet before his feathers have grown, won't you, Annabel? If it rains while you're out swimming together perhaps you ought to put an arm over him just as if it were your wing.'

Annabel and Dalton looked at each other.

'I see,' said Annabel.

'Oh, it's exciting, isn't it?' breathed Miss Ballantyne with a sudden delicious little sigh. 'I really quite envy you, Annabel.'

Miss Ballantyne was right. Teaching Dalton to swim *was* the demanding part. Every morning before school, wet or fine, cold or warm, Annabel had to take him down to the river. The duckpond had been ruled out as being too shallow, muddy and smelly to be practical but there was a pool in the river, just downstream from the bridge, which was calm and sheltered and just right.

Annabel would lower herself shivering into the

water and set off, followed at a short distance by a cheerful-looking Dalton, who appeared to regard it as the most enjoyable part of the day. She would swim with steady strokes almost up to the bridge, then turn in a half-circle and make her way back again, blue with cold.

A small crowd, chiefly composed of boys from Lord Willoughby's, would gather on the bridge to make quacking noises and throw lumps of stale bread. Kate, loyal as ever, would be ready with a big towel when she emerged.

'I sh-shall be gggglad when you're b-big-big enough to go solo,' grumbled Annabel, teeth chattering.

But Kate noticed that Annabel wasn't really grumbling very much, not half as much as she would have expected.

Dalton's devotion became only more intense. As he grew bigger, which he did with great speed, he took it for granted that he should be allowed to follow Annabel everywhere and she seemed quite happy to let him.

She was even allowed to take him to school, Miss Ballantyne having managed to persuade the Headmaster, Mr Trimm, that it would be in the interests of science.

'So this is the famous duck I've been hearing about!' beamed Mr Trimm, meeting Annabel and Dalton in the corridor one day. 'Do we have a name for him?'

'Dalton,' replied Annabel. 'Dalton Bunce.'

'An unusual name. May I ask why you called him that?'

Before Annabel could reply, Mr Dalton appeared from round a corner, frowning over some exercise books he was flicking through, and Mr Trimm's gaze went to him.

10

'What about his feeding programme?' said the Headmaster, turning swiftly back to Annabel. 'Do you have any difficulties?'

'You must admit I'm a good mother,' Annabel said proudly to Kate one day as they watched Dalton pottering around the garden. 'He's growing up into such a big, strong, healthy duck.'

'Too big and strong,' said Mrs Bunce from her deck chair. 'He ought to be out on the pond with the other ducks. He can't stay here all alone for ever.'

'I know that perfectly well, mum,' said Annabel. 'I'm just as keen for him to get back to the pond as you are.'

'I thought you seemed to be getting quite fond of him,' said Kate.

'Just because I put up with it without grumbling all the time doesn't mean I've changed my mind about him,' replied Annabel, looking martyred. 'I just can't wait to have my freedom again. I dream of the day when I'll be able to go somewhere without having a duck following me around.'

Two days later, on a Saturday afternoon, it seemed that Annabel's dream might soon be realized.

Annabel and Kate had taken Dalton for a long walk in the country but while they were still two miles from Addendon on the way back a passing bus looked inviting and Annabel waved it down.

Having climbed aboard, they stood on the platform waiting for Dalton to hop on as he had learnt to do. 'Come on, Dalton, get a move on,' said Annabel as he lingered. 'Jump aboard like a good duck – Hey!'

The cry was because the bus had started off again with a jerk just as Dalton was gathering himself. Unfortunately the driver hadn't realized he was there.

11

Dalton's leap ended in mid-air with a quack and a flap. As the bus roared off round a bend in the road, Annabel and Kate caught a heart-rending glimpse of him trying to regain his balance.

'Dalton!' screamed Annabel, yanking at the bell rope. 'Stop! You've left Dalton behind!'

But the bus kept on going. Presumably the driver, concentrating on the road, thought that the bell was being rung in anticipation of the next stop along. The front seat passenger stared at Annabel.

'There wasn't anybody else there,' he said, 'I could see.'

'My son!' screamed Annabel.

By the time the bus came to a halt it had travelled a considerable distance. Annabel ran all the way back. Panting after her, Kate reflected that she didn't seem as pleased as all that not to have Dalton following her around.

There was no sign of Dalton. Not a trace.

'Dalton!' yelled Annabel, looking rather like a panic-stricken duck herself as she raced hither and thither in search of him. 'Dalton, where are you? It's me – mother. Come back to mother!'

There was no answering quack.

Luckily, no cars had passed so he couldn't have been run over. It was unlikely a fox could have been so quick off the mark, especially in daylight. So he must have gone into the woods which lay on either side of the road. But which direction had he taken?

Annabel was distraught. Almost until darkness fell she ransacked the woods and fields that lay beyond.

'But Annabel,' Kate said once, as she stumbled after her, 'I thought you were *hoping* to get rid of Dalton. I thought you couldn't wait to go to places without having him follow you around.'

Annabel didn't seem to hear. In the end, Kate

almost had to drag her away because her parents would be getting worried.

'But I'm going to find him, Kate,' she said, as they boarded the bus home. 'You don't have to come back here tomorrow but I'm going to. I'm his mother and he can't live without me. He'll just mope and pine away. I'll never stop searching until I find him.'

Kate thought the chances were almost nil but it would have been no use telling Annabel that. On the following morning, Sunday, they went back to the spot on their bikes.

And, amazingly, they did find Dalton. It was mid-morning and Annabel, exhausted but indomitable, had hobbled to a farm gate to rest for a few moments before continuing the search. Kate leaned against it with her.

Some geese, cackling in the farmyard behind them, caused them to look round. And suddenly Annabel's exhaustion dropped away.

'Dalton!' she squealed.

A girl of about the same age as Annabel and Kate was walking across the farmyard towards an open-sided barn with some bales of hay stacked in it. A duck was waddling in her wake. He was the picture of devotion, pausing when she paused for a moment, moving on when she moved on.

Annabel was through the gate like a flash.

Kate would have had no idea whether it was Dalton or not. As far as she was concerned, it could have been any duck. But Annabel seemed to have no doubt whatsoever and, after all, a mother should know her own child.

'Dalton,' said Annabel, in a voice that quivered, 'Dalton, it's me – mother.'

The girl had started to break up a bale of hay. She

turned and looked at Annabel in surprise. So did Dalton.

'Is he yours?' asked the girl, as Annabel scooped him passionately up. 'He turned up this morning and he's been following me round ever since. I don't mind but if he's yours do take him.'

So it *was* Dalton. Annabel's maternal instinct had not been at fault. Kate was impressed.

She looked at the girl. 'You look a bit like Annabel,' she said. 'Perhaps that's why he decided to follow you around.' The girl looked bewildered.

'Well, you've got your real mother back again,' cooed Annabel, nursing Dalton dotingly. 'Have you been missing me? Haz-oo been a-pining for me? You're safe again now – safe with mother and you're coming right back home with me.'

'Yes, do take him,' said the startled farm girl. Kate started humming softly to herself, gazing at far horizons and pretending she'd never seen Annabel before in her life.

'I'll get on with my work,' said the farm girl, picking up some of the hay and backing away. 'I'm glad you've got your – er – your duck back.'

But things weren't to be quite as simple as that. For the instant Annabel put Dalton down on the ground again, he waddled off after the farm girl.

'Dalton!' screeched Annabel, blankly astonished. 'Dalton, come back!'

Dalton didn't look round.

Annabel trotted after him, arms outstretched pleadingly, tears starting to run slowly down her face.

'Dalton – I brought you up, didn't I? I took you out for early morning swims. I made you a big strong duckling. Dalton, remember everything we've done together. I'm your mother.'

Dalton didn't care. The last Kate saw of him, he

was trailing after the farm girl, pausing when she paused, moving on again when she moved on. Annabel was yesterday's mother.

After the first shock, Annabel took her loss bravely and, for once, didn't flaunt her grief. It was too big for that.

'In fact, Kate,' she said as they arrived back in front of her house, a quivering lip the only sign of the emotions raging within her, 'you know I've been hoping something like this would happen. I told you that, didn't I? It's all for the best. He'll be so much happier growing up on a farm, where I expect there's a pond and the company of other ducks when he wants it. I couldn't offer him everything a growing duck should have. I'm – I'm –'

Annabel seemed to be having difficulty with her speech.

'– anyway you know what a nuisance he was becoming and how I've been dying to get rid of him –'

She had turned her face away from Kate and the words were coming out in a sort of howl.

'– I'm so glad things have turned out this way but I'd like to be alone now.'

Kate, a loyal friend, understood.

Who dunnit?

*****

'Now what,' said Mrs Muriel da Susa M A (Oxon), B Sc (Soc.) (London), Adv. Dip. Ed. (London), Deputy Head of Lord Willoughby's School, 'what makes Addendon Rovers such an excellent side? We all know, don't we? It's *character*.'

3G regarded her numbly.

'When they're one-nil down because of some diabolical decision by the ref, when they're being crucified by the fans even though they know they've been using all their skills, what is it that enables them still to put it all together and produce their magic? It's *character*.'

'What's she talking about?' whispered Annabel.

'Football,' Kate whispered back. 'She's trying to get through to us in a language we can understand. She must have a message for us.'

'Oh,' said Annabel. 'Something about team spirit and not letting the side down, I expect.'

It was Monday morning in the classroom and Mrs da Susa was supposed to be giving 3G an RE lesson but she seemed to have other things on her mind. She was unfolding a piece of notepaper on the desk in front of her. Her long, lean, rather manly face bore its normal expression of suffering.

16

Mrs da Susa liked to talk in terms which she thought her pupils would understand – usually references to subjects such as football or pop music – even if she herself didn't. She felt that it brought her close to them. It was a habit which drove Mr Trimm, the Headmaster, mad but then it was common knowledge that most things about Mrs da Susa drove him mad. He himself was of the 'old school', looking back nostalgically to good healthy canings for the boys when required and, for the girls, the copying out of immensely long, turgid pieces of prose.

Whereas Mrs da Susa, although she didn't look it, considered herself to be of the 'new school', believing in understanding, psychology, getting to the root of the problem and, if all else failed, the withdrawal of privileges. She was, in other words, a fairly soft touch.

'I have here,' she continued now, 'a letter which must be one of the most humiliating I –'

She paused as she saw that Miles Noggins had put his hand up, presumably to ask a question. This was such an incredibly unusual event that she didn't want to discourage him.

'Yes, Miles?' she asked.

'Please, Miss,' he said. 'Addendon Rovers aren't a good side. They're terrible. Their goalie's useless.'

'The whole team's useless,' muttered Richard White. 'They're second from bottom of the league.'

There were murmurings of agreement from the knowledgeable.

Annabel listened with mild interest. She herself, like Kate, was hardly aware that Addendon had a football team. She was dimly conscious of it only occasionally when, if happening to walk along Station Road on a winter Saturday afternoon, she might hear some vague roarings and stampings and shouts of 'C'mon the Rovers' from the other side of a long, high board fence. It would make her feel <u>chilly</u> and <u>wintry</u> and she would hurry on.

'We'll talk about the Rovers in more detail some other time,' said Mrs da Susa. 'At the moment I want to discuss this letter. As I was saying, it's humiliating, humiliating.'

She closed her eyes for a moment in grief, a habit of hers.

'It's from the proprietor of the Buntingbury Tropical Bird Park, where, you will remember, a party of us had such an enjoyable time just two or three months ago.'

Annabel remembered. Yes, it had been fun there. Why on earth should the proprietor be writing Mrs da Susa humiliating letters? You'd think he'd be one of the few people she'd come into contact with who'd have no need . . .

'A few days ago I wrote again to the Bird Park, telling them how much we'd enjoyed it and saying that I would be bringing another party, mainly from 3H, in about a fortnight's time. In reply I received this.'

Mrs da Susa paused.

'I don't propose – I can't – read you the entire letter. To put it briefly, they are asking that before I bring any more parties from this school I must give them an undertaking that – that the party will be under proper control and that there will be no repetition of what happened on our last visit . . .'

There was some murmuring and <u>shuffling</u> amongst the class.

'What *did* happen?' whispered Kate. 'I don't remember anything.'

'Neither do I,' said Annabel, <u>mystified</u>.

'I can see that most of you are puzzled,' said Mrs da Susa. 'Like me, you hadn't realized that anything

18

went amiss on our visit. There was nothing to spoil what was a thoroughly happy afternoon. Alas! Apparently it wasn't until after we'd gone that it came to light.'

She paused significantly.

'However, when I describe what happened, it may be that there will be a guilty start of recognition from someone in the class. Perhaps that someone already knows what I'm about to say. If so, perhaps he or she would like to put their hand up now.'

There were no takers. Mrs da Susa looked down at the letter again.

'Very well. It appears that, after we had left, the proprietor discovered that someone had released one of his most valuable birds, a –' she peered – 'a *Satyr Tragopan*, from its enclosure. The gate had been deliberately opened and left ajar. Now he's quite certain it was one of us because we were the only people there at the time and only twenty minutes before we left he'd noticed that the gate was quite secure. I suppose that whoever did this thought it was an amusing thing to do.'

Mrs da Susa looked up again, perhaps hoping that some guilt-ridden hand would now be raising itself. If so, she was disappointed. She sighed and continued.

'The *Satyr Tragopan* comes, it seems, from the Himalayas. It's a round, plump bird the size of a cockerel which has a skulking, scratching habit. This was, I gather, a male bird which has a quite spectacular plumage, rusty red in colour with a white spot in the middle of every feather.

'Now it seems that the bird had completely disappeared and that there was considerable alarm. Searches had to be started both in the surrounding countryside and in the Bird Park itself, which, you will recall, is thickly wooded and a very easy place for a bird to hide in. No trace of it was found that day and it wasn't until the following morning that it was seen scratching in one of the gardens in the nearby village. Although pursued, it managed to escape. There were several other sightings that day but each time it managed to evade capture. Being a valuable bird, its wings were pinioned but even so it appears to have been quite far-ranging and elusive.

'It wasn't until the late afternoon that it was caught and then only because it appeared in the village tea-rooms while a party from a Darby and Joan Club were having a cream tea there. It made a considerable nuisance of itself scratching and rummaging around the tables before leaping on to the tables themselves and spoiling several cream teas. I gather that some of the ladies were very alarmed and left the tea-rooms, quite understandably since they had never seen anything like it before and couldn't be certain that it would not be aggressive. Fortunately, the proprietor of the Bird Park then arrived and was able to recapture it. It had by then been at liberty for about twenty-four hours.

'So *that*,' said Mrs da Susa, martyrdom in her voice, 'is the shame we have to live with and for which I now have to apologize ignominiously before I can take another party there.'

There was a coarse snigger from somewhere near the back of the room which Mrs da Susa either didn't hear or ignored if she did. It appeared to come from Damian Price and Kate noticed that Annabel turned her head and glared at him indignantly.

'I hope,' said Mrs da Susa, 'that now that the full extent of what happened has been made known to you, the guilty person will have the decency to come forward and own up.'

She looked around but still no one moved.

Annabel looked round, too, rather quickly it seemed to Kate, as if she were hoping to catch some flicker of guilt on someone's face, some downcast eye that was not prepared to look up and meet that of Mrs da Susa. So Kate looked round as well.

There was nothing of that nature to be seen. Miles Noggins was gazing open-mouthed into space, like some old gentleman asleep and snoring in an armchair, but that was perfectly usual. Justine Bird's eyes were downcast. But that appeared to be because she was doing her fingernails under cover of the desk. Sheena Franks-Walters gazed sweetly and enigmatically at Mrs da Susa but that was her normal posture, too.

Otherwise, 3G had taken Mrs da Susa's revelations with calmness and complacency, even a little derision.

'Sounds as if the *Satyr Tragopan* had quite a jolly day,' said Kate to Annabel as they both turned their faces to the front again.

Annabel, however, didn't seem to agree. She looked quite cross.

'Poor little thing,' she said, 'being chased round all day. It must have been hungry to have gone into those tea-rooms and then all those people frightened it. For once I've got some sympathy with Mrs da Susa, as well. She went to the trouble to organize that outing for us and we let her down –'

Mrs da Susa had not, however, finished. She was holding up a large photograph.

'You'll remember, of course,' she said, 'that this picture of the whole party was taken just as we were about to leave the Bird Park. Most of you have copies. It's ironic to think that someone in this happy group had, only minutes before, been betraying us, that the Judas in our midst is depicted right here.'

21

Her voice became a little shrill.

'I expect that person to own up and I hope he or she will have the grace to do so by tomorrow. There is no room in our team for the professional tackler, the fouler, the one who has to be shown the yellow card. But own up and I shall be over the moon – is something the matter, Annabel?'

Annabel had been nodding vigorously.

'I was just agreeing with you, Mrs da Susa,' she said. She hesitated, searching for a phrase. She had heard another muffled snigger from the back of the room and she wanted to show Mrs da Susa that the whole of 3G wasn't without finer feelings. For once, incredibly, she felt like identifying with her.

'Good skills!' said Annabel. Although she didn't know what it meant it sounded like a football phrase and it would show Mrs da Susa that she was on her side.

It didn't matter that Annabel didn't know what it meant because Mrs da Susa didn't know either. But she, too, recognized it as a football phrase. To her it appeared simply that at long last her attempts to get into the hearts and minds of her pupils were bearing a little fruit. Annabel Bunce, of all people, was responding.

It was a moment of joy for Mrs da Susa. In a rare meeting of minds, the two ignoramuses looked favourably upon each other.

It was also the moment when Annabel, indignant at the plight in which the *Satyr Tragopan* had found itself and in her mood of warm sympathy towards Mrs da Susa, made her resolve.

She would find the villain in this case and put it to him or her plainly that, for the good of the team, it was their duty to confess.

Yes, she, Annabel, was going to investigate the crime.

It was, as Annabel informed Kate that evening, a fascinating challenge. She was quite excited by it.

'Because, you see, Kate,' she said, 'this is a mystery that we've got to solve just from any clues we can find in a group photograph. It's the only way. And maybe it's the first time it's ever been done. Maybe even Scotland Yard have never tried it.'

'Do you think it's possible?' asked Kate doubtfully.

'Anything is possible if you put a mind to it,' said Annabel.

The photograph in question, a copy of the one that Mrs da Susa had produced, taken at the Bird Park, was sellotaped to the wall of Annabel's bedroom. Annabel carefully took it down, placed it on her little table and drew up two chairs, one for herself, the other for Kate.

'And, anyway,' she continued, sitting down, 'it has to be. Anybody who's kept the secret as long as this isn't going to lose their head and give the game away now. But the picture was taken straight after it was done. There must be some clue in it, even if it's only somebody looking flustered. We've got to be logical, Kate, think like real detectives, use psychoanalysis.'

Kate sat down too and looked at the picture. She remained doubtful. Though, certainly, there seemed to be no other way. Annabel had made some inquiries amongst 3G during the day and got nowhere. It had all been so long ago.

The picture showed the school party standing beside the coach which was just about to take them home. Close by was a large sign saying BUNTING-BURY TROPICAL BIRD PARK. In the background a broad path, overhung by trees and dappled with

23

sunlight and shade, curved into the heart of the Bird Park. About half of 3G had gone on the outing together with a few teachers, including, of course, Mrs da Susa herself.

'We have to get this sorted out quickly,' said Annabel, 'because I've still got some homework to do. We'll make a list of suspects giving them a number of stars according to how suspicious they are. Got a biro?'

'Here,' said Kate.

'Now what strikes me as strange, first of all,' continued Annabel, 'is that whoever committed the crime has managed to keep quiet about it all this time.'

'Good point, Annabel,' nodded Kate.

'It's out of character. I can imagine Damian Price doing it, for instance, but he'd have been boasting about it all the way home. He wouldn't have been able to keep quiet. That applies to any of the obvious suspects. I can't help feeling that this is very significant; that if we find the answer to that puzzle, we find the criminal.'

Kate was nodding again. She was impressed. 'That's very shrewd, Annabel,' she said.

'Yes, I think there's more to this case than meets the eye,' said Annabel, thoughtfully, 'a lot more.' She got up and paced the room a couple of times excitedly before sitting down again. 'I have a feeling that we're not dealing here with one of the regulars, the normal small fry. There's a bigger brain behind this. So let's start looking at some *unlikely* ones, somebody with brains, perhaps.'

'Deborah Breakspear?' suggested Kate. 'Or Julian, perhaps.'

Deborah was *very* unlikely. She was also fearfully brainy and every term competed with Julian Parlane

24

to come top of the class. She was in the middle of the front row of the picture while Julian was in the second row on the right.

As some sort of penance for being so brainy, Deborah ought to have been plain, gauche and physically maladjusted but instead she was pretty, poised in a shy sort of way and good at games.

She didn't have a regular best friend, being too busy studying, but she had chummed up with one or two people at different times and Annabel had been struck by what she regarded as an interesting phenomenon, namely that during the course of their friendships with her both of these girls – Tracey Cooke and Angela Dill – had moved up a few notches in term order.

Annabel had theorized from this that it was possible for Deborah's braininess to rub off on anyone who was regularly in close contact with her and had herself made overtures of friendship, somewhat to Deborah's surprise.

It hadn't in fact worked in Annabel's case. Instead, association with Annabel had caused Deborah's own performance to falter and she had been beaten to a poor second that term by Julian. Nevertheless others had concluded that there might be something in Annabel's theory and Deborah was still puzzled by the way people kept on pushing themselves upon her and giving her things.

'It's just possible,' said Annabel, dubiously, 'that she had a sudden wild desire to kick over the traces. That she got fed up with being good for so long. Or that Julian did.'

But she had to admit that their expressions didn't give any support to the theory. They seemed *too* unlikely. Not even one-star suspects. Not even a star between them.

'Miles Noggins has got a funny expression on his face, hasn't he?' said Kate, who was becoming interested in this psychoanalysis of 3G.

'You're right, Kate,' said Annabel. 'Perhaps you're on to something there.'

Miles Noggins was standing close behind Justine Bird and peering over her shoulder. These two were at the other end of the intellectual scale from Deborah and Julian, fighting their sluggish, slow-motion battle for bottom place in term order. Miles had little concern for academic matters. He was more of a gourmet, his interests being chiefly food and drink – especially crisps, chips, sweets, and the like – and avoiding games, for which his stout, ungainly figure was admittedly not built.

Justine's range of interests was less wide, being confined to boys. (Though definitely not Third Year boys and preferably not Willers boys at all. She preferred them to be older, working, with money or, at a pinch, unemployed, with money.)

'Justine's got a funny expression on her face, too,' said Kate, thoughtfully.

'You're right again, Kate,' said Annabel. 'You're so observant.'

Indeed, Justine's face, normally impassive save for the motions of chewing gum, wore quite an animated expression.

'No, I see the reason,' said Annabel. 'Look. Look closely. She's grinding her heel down Miles's shin. That accounts for both their expressions.'

'Oh, yes,' said Kate. 'Yes. I suppose he'd trod on her heel or something. That's just what he would do.'

So that was that.

'Sheena Franks-Walters!' said Annabel, suddenly stabbing her finger on a girl who stood to one side and very slightly apart from the group, a sweetly enigmatic smile on her face, 'She's a possibility, isn't she?'

Sheena Franks-Walters was something of an enigma to the rest of 3G. Innumerable were the discussions that had been held about her, endless the speculation as to precisely why she sat there in a desk by herself, in the front row at the side of the classroom, a sweet expression on her round, dimpled face as she gazed benignly at whoever was teaching.

The great puzzle about her was that her parents were the owners of Addendon Court, a vast estate in the country about a mile outside Addendon, and phenomenally wealthy. So why would they send her to Willers? Who would send their daughter there from choice? It wasn't as if she were learning anything, anyway. Only an apparently instinctive knowledge of English grammar, picked up at home, kept her slightly ahead of Miles and Justine.

Imaginative people said she was a spy for the Education Authority. Cruel people said she was too thick. Kinder ones said that the thickness was simulated, though having to admit that if so it was a very good act.

Sheena continued to sit with the sweet expression on her face, rising slowly and deliberately when necessary to go for breaks and meals – she invariably brought her own packed lunch of smoked salmon sandwiches, various patés and cheeses, prepared for her by the cook at Addendon Court – saying please and thank you in a graciously upper-class manner if someone actually refrained from slamming a door in her face but otherwise making no contact.

The sweetly placid look remained even when some people called her 'Sheena Frankly-Awful' to her face, instead of merely behind her back, hoping to get a reaction out of her.

They were invariably disappointed. At four o'clock, Sheena would pad serenely out of school and step into a large chauffeur-driven car to be taken back to her other life with Mummy and Daddy at Addendon Court.

It was one of Annabel's small ambitions that some day she would crack that sweet smile and resolve the enigma of Sheena Frankly-Awf –, of Sheena Franks-Walters.

But could she be behind the mystery of the *Satyr Tragopan*? Annabel put her down as a two-star suspect and passed on, moving her finger slowly across the photograph.

It stopped on Julia Channing. Kate knew that Annabel would have liked to pin the crime on to Julia Channing because they seldom saw eye to eye. Annabel considered Julia to be a boaster and a snob. Julia was the one person who hung around Sheena Franks-Walters hoping to become friendly with her and get invited to Addendon Court. So far, to her credit, Sheena didn't appear to have noticed her.

Annabel's eyes hovered upon her for a moment, then reluctantly moved on.

'She wouldn't have the nerve,' she said and crossed out the star she had started to draw.

'I've just noticed,' said Kate, startled. 'What is Mr Rumator doing there?'

She had spotted the tall, shy figure of the Lord Willoughby's groundsman standing in the shadow of the school coach.

'Oh, I invited him along,' said Annabel carelessly. 'He loves birds. I told him that if he sat in the back Mrs da Susa wouldn't notice.'

Mr Rumator was a great friend of Annabel's. They would spend many hours in earnest discussion, Kate had no idea what about. Annabel simply said that he was the one person at Willers from whom she got any real education.

'Yes,' said Annabel, 'the more you look into this picture, the more you see, don't you?'

'Hmm,' said Kate. She wasn't going to dismiss Mr Rumator as easily as that. A thought had occurred to her.

So Mr Rumator loved birds! It could be that he was someone who had strong feelings about keeping birds in captivity. He might be just the sort. Supposing . . . it would explain a lot if *he* had done it.

But it wasn't any use saying that to Annabel, whose detection was probably not entirely unbiased and who almost certainly wouldn't hear a word against Mr Rumator.

Without Annabel noticing, Kate slid another piece of paper in front of her, wrote 'Mr Rumator' on it, and placed three stars by his name. She could have a suspect of her own.

'This is getting quite exciting, Annabel,' she said. 'I'm beginning to think you're right. Maybe we'll find the criminal.'

'Something I've been noticing,' said Annabel, 'is how many teachers went on this trip. Six including Mrs da Susa. It's unusual for so many to go on an outing like this. I wonder – could it be significant?'

'I'm trying to remember,' said Kate, frowning. 'Wasn't Mr Trimm giving a lecture at school that afternoon. Maybe –'

'Supposing,' said Annabel, not paying any attention whatsoever, 'supposing it were a *teacher* that committed the crime.'

Annabel found that a really exciting thought. She got up and had another pace on the strength of it, then sat down again.

'Motive, Kate, that's what we've got to think

about, motive. Now just look at the way Mr Rogers is looking at Mr Polegate behind Miss Ballantyne's back.'

The three teachers stood in a row, a sweetly-smiling Miss Ballantyne in the middle. Certainly it looked as if Mr Rogers were casting a somewhat bad-tempered glance at Mr Polegate.

'It's obvious why those three went on the outing,' said Annabel. 'Miss Ballantyne is interested in birds and Mr Polegate and Mr Rogers are interested in Miss Ballantyne and wanted to keep an eye on each other. Supposing . . .'

She brooded.

'Supposing it's a crime of passion. Supposing Mr Rogers had let that bird out hoping that Mr Polegate would be accused of the crime and his name blackened in Miss Ballantyne's eyes.'

'It wasn't a very successful plan, was it,' Kate pointed out.

'We know he's ruthless,' said Annabel, reluctant to give up the idea. 'We know he cheats when he's refereeing matches with other schools. Perhaps for a moment, when standing by the bird's enclosure, he was consumed with a sudden, fierce hatred of Mr Polegate that was too much to bear. Before he could stop to think he'd let the bird out, then instantly regretted what he'd done. But it was too late. That might be quite a likely explanation, Kate.'

'Hmm,' said Kate, dubiously, 'I think he might just be glancing about him, you know.' Her money was still on Mr Rumator.

'Well, I'm keeping him as suspect number one for the time being,' said Annabel, firmly giving him four stars. 'You know, I think we're beginning to get somewhere – Kate, look! Look who's there in the background.'

30

'Mr da Susa!' exclaimed Kate. 'I'd forgotten all about him going.'

'So had I!' said Annabel. 'It just shows you, doesn't it? It's no good relying on memory. You've got to have *evidence*.'

Mr da Susa was, of course, Mrs da Susa's husband. He was loafing in the background of the picture in the shade of some trees, hands in pockets. He was at present unemployed and tending to hang around the school or, to Mrs da Susa's even greater embarrassment, accompany her on outings.

He was an agreeable and engaging Italian whom Mrs da Susa had met many years ago while on holiday in that country. It had been the one romantic interlude in her life. He had been following her around because he thought she was some other girl and only realized his mistake after effecting an introduction by pretending to save her from a non-existent bus which wasn't really about to run her over.

However, he had gallantly not let on. One thing had led to another and now here he was, a long established resident of Addendon, loafing around at odd jobs while Mrs da Susa, after a gruelling day as Deputy Head of Willers, came home to cook his meals.

She had tried to explain to him about Women's Lib but the explanation had left him puzzled and his English had failed him as it tended to in moments of stress. He thought that Women's Lib was about women having jobs *and* running the home. Wasn't that what they wanted? Wasn't it what they'd always fought for?

Mrs da Susa had come to terms with the fact that it was impossible to keep him in order. Both the men in her life, her husband and Mr Trimm, were incorrigible.

'Supposing it's a cry for help,' said Annabel.

'Cry for help?' repeated Kate. 'Who from? Why?'

'From Mr da Susa. Supposing he can't stand any longer seeing his wife busy and successful while he's out of work. Anyway, fancy having to live with somebody domineering like her! Always bossing you around and trying to understand you! We can get away from her but he can't.'

'He looks as if he's humming and smiling to himself,' said Kate, doubtfully. 'That's the sort of expression that's on his face.'

Annabel stared at the photograph, unconvinced.

Mainly to take her mind off Mr da Susa, Kate said:

'There are two other teachers there, Mr Ribbons and Mrs Jesty. What about them? They both look a bit tight-lipped, don't they, as if they've got something on their minds.'

'Oh, I expect they've been quarrelling as usual,' said Annabel, whose mind was reverting to Mr Rogers. She looked at them. They were standing one on either side of Mrs da Susa. 'Still, I suppose we'd better consider them.'

Mr Ribbons (or 'Red' Ribbons as he was sometimes known because of his political views) was their physics master and sported a spade beard and rimless spectacles. The rumour was that the beard was false and the spectacles had plain-glass lenses and that he only wore them to create a certain image.

Whether that were so or not, he was certainly very forward in his thinking, particularly in his attitude to Authority, which he saw it as his duty to undermine. To that end he operated as a sort of staff-room 'mole', giving his classes a great deal of information about the private lives of Mr Trimm, Mrs da Susa and other teachers in the belief that it would encourage them to treat that Authority with the Contempt it deserved.

It was largely thanks to him that, in the noble cause of the coming revolution, the pupils of Lord Willoughby's were aware, on any given day, whether the da Susas had had a row the night before or whether Mr Trimm had run out of clean black socks.

His own private life remained a total mystery.

Otherwise he occasionally distributed political literature surreptitiously in the classroom and, curiously, there seemed to be some sort of unspoken rapport between him and Sheena Franks-Walters.

Mrs Jesty, the senior history teacher, a kindly, dithering, grey-haired lady, was Chairman of the Addendon Conservatives and his arch-enemy. They quarrelled endlessly. They would quarrel over whether the staff-room window should be open or closed, over which brand of polish should be used for the school floors, anything which was quarrelable about. Annabel maintained that they enjoyed it and certainly they seemed to seek each other's company.

'I suppose,' said Annabel now, 'that it's just possible that Mr Ribbons might have let the bird out as some sort of blow against society –' she paused as a thought struck her – 'Kate, what colour was the bird? I've forgotten.'

'Rusty red,' replied Kate. 'With white spots on.'

'Rusty red!' repeated Annabel, with excitement. 'That might be significant. He might have felt a sudden sort of solidarity with it – you know, that they were brothers – and had this impulse to give it its liberty.'

The excitement faded as quickly as it had come.

'No,' said Annabel, simply.

She stared at the photograph, brooding. After a considerable time, she said, without emotion: 'Kate, I think I've spotted the villain.'

'You have?' said Kate, startled by the suddenness of it.

'Yes, but I'll need a magnifying glass to make sure. I've got one somewhere here.'

Annabel got up and started to rummage around in a drawer.

'But who?' asked Kate.

'It's really quite amazing. I don't think you're going to believe this when I tell you.'

'But *who*?'

'Mrs da Susa.'

'Mrs *da Susa*?'

'I said you wouldn't believe it, didn't I? But isn't it always the way? The most unlikely person turns out to be the murderer. Just like a whodunnit.'

Annabel was still rummaging around in the drawer.

'Look, Kate. Look at the expression on Mrs da Susa's face and what it is she's glancing at out of the corner of her eye. Follow the line of her gaze. There's something there in the bushes, isn't there, *something that could be a bird*, skulking, scratching perhaps. And she *knows*, doesn't she, Kate? She's guilty about it – look!'

Kate peered, doubtfully.

'I suppose it *could* be a bird. It's difficult to say. It *might* be a piece of paper. You're right about her looking at it, though. But, Annabel, if it is the bird and she knew it was free and didn't let on, that would mean – oh, I just don't believe it.'

Annabel had found the magnifying glass. She pounced on the picture again.

'Why not? She's absent-minded. Let's reconstruct the crime – try and visualize it. Supposing – just supposing Kate that, say, Mrs da Susa collects birds' feathers for a hobby. Supposing she saw a

34

feather lying in the bird's enclosure and was tempted.

'Picture it, Kate. Stealthily she looks around her to make sure no one's about. She unbolts the gate, nips inside and picks up the feather. And then, in her excitement and haste as she leaves the enclosure, she forgets to see that the bolt is properly home again. The gate swings open . . .'

Annabel paused. She was standing, holding the picture in her hand, now examining it through the magnifying glass.

'I don't find that all that easy to visualize,' said Kate, half closing her eyes as she tried to do so. 'In fact, it's quite difficult but I suppose it's possible –'

She noticed that a curious expression was now crossing Annabel's face. It was really a very odd look and most difficult to interpret. Annabel was still peering through the magnifying glass.

'Well?' asked Kate. 'Is it?'

'Is it what?' said Annabel, abstractedly.

'The bird. The *Satyr Tragopan*. The thing in the bushes that Mrs da Susa's looking at.'

'Oh, *that*,' said Annabel. 'No. I made a mistake. I think that's some old piece of brown paper blowing about – probably a sandwich wrapping. You know how Mrs da Susa hates litter. I expect her husband dropped it and she was furious.'

'Then –'

'Do keep quiet a minute, Kate. I'm trying to see something else.'

After another few moments, she lowered the magnifying glass. When she spoke again, she appeared to be choosing her words very carefully.

'We hadn't,' she said, 'actually considered every-one in the picture. While, as it happened, I proved to be wrong about Mrs da Susa, the magnifying glass does reveal something else, something rather important.'

As she was speaking Kate noticed something which had previously escaped her attention, although it was little more than an arm's length away from her.

Annabel's room was littered with evidence of her hobbies, past and present. The walls were covered with photographs and pictures, shelves were strewn with pressed flowers, stamp albums, sea and snail shells, coloured pebbles from beaches, cheap jewellery . . . if it were collectable, Annabel had at some time collected it.

On the shelf beside Kate was Annabel's collection of bird's feathers. Prominent amongst them was a rusty red one with a white spot in the middle. It was extremely pretty.

'Annabel!' said Kate, startled.

'Yes, Kate,' continued Annabel hollowly – she didn't appear to have heard her – 'Mrs de Susa can be cleared. But the magnifying glass has revealed, without any shadow of doubt, the real villain in this affair.'

She gave a little wriggle of embarrassment.

'Me.'

Kate picked up the magnifying glass and looked at the picture through it. She saw what Annabel meant.

Annabel stood, smiling brightly, right in the foreground of the picture. In her hand was clutched something which was revealed by the magnifying glass to be a bird's feather, doubtless the same feather which was now on the shelf beside her.

'Yes,' said Annabel and then again, 'yes. It comes back to me now. My reconstruction of the crime was in fact absolutely right. It was quite a brilliant piece of deduction in a way. The enclosure was in fact

36

opened by someone tempted to sneak in and pick up a very attractive feather which was lying on the ground. And then, so delighted was this person with the feather that she absent-mindedly forgot to close the gate . . . it's just that the identity of the – er – the actual person wasn't quite – not quite –'

She sighed and looked at the feather on the shelf.

'You must admit it's very beautiful, Kate.'

'Yes,' said Kate, laying the magnifying glass aside. 'What'll you do now, Annabel?'

'I shall own up in the morning, of course,' said Annabel. Her chin lifted. 'It'll be a proud moment for Mrs da Susa when she sees that the team is pulling together, that her words have had an effect. Yes, she'll be really pleased. I'm looking forward to that.'

The look of embarrassment was already disappearing. 'Yes,' she said, quite brightly, 'a fine piece of detective work even if we do say so ourselves. I told you we'd do it, Kate, didn't I? Not many people would have pulled that off.'

Annabel was, by now, looking extremely pleased with herself. She put the magnifying glass away, stuck the picture back on the wall and gave the feather a little stroke.

'Like I said to Mrs da Susa only this morning: *Good skills!*'

Annabel and the Third Year disco

*****

'It's so difficult, isn't it?' shouted Julia Channing. 'Impossible, really. I mean I don't want to hurt anybody's feelings but what can I do when I've got four boys pestering me? *Four!* I can't invite all of them, can I?'

'I know, I know,' yelled Tracey Cooke. 'I've got exactly the same problem. Bound to offend somebody. Beginning to wish we'd never started the whole thing.'

Her words had a staccato, radio-message-like quality about them. They bounced off the school building and went echoing off into space, signals to distant worlds.

'Boasters!' fumed Annabel, listening.

'Don't pay any attention,' hissed Kate, soothingly. 'It's just bragging. You don't care about it, do you? It's pathetic, isn't it?'

'Absolutely and utterly paTHETic!'

'Then think about something else. What about telling me why your parents gave you Fidelity as a middle name, for instance? You're always promising –'

'Just wait till I can boast back at *them*. Just wait.'

Annabel was very much on edge. It was the lunch

break at Lord Willoughby's and she and Kate had been sitting on the grass reasonably contentedly until Julia and Tracey had come strolling along behind them to remind them of the Third Year disco, which was now only eight days away.

The disco was being organized by the girls of 3G themselves. The original conception had been that it would be a pleasurable occasion to which everyone concerned could look forward. Perhaps when the evening actually arrived that would turn out to be the case. Anything was possible. But at present it was an irrelevance which was no longer occurring to anyone except possibly Justine Bird of the sultry manner and string of genuine boy friends.

For everyone else it had merely produced a struggle for status. Because, for this disco, it had been decided that each girl had to produce a boy and definitely not a Third Year boy.

There had been general agreement that the Third Year boys wouldn't be any use. One or two of them had a thin veneer of sophistication but even in the best cases it was very thin indeed and savagery, if not actually on the surface, was very close to it. It showed itself in their interests, which tended to be nothing more inspiring than electronics, airguns, fighting and the like.

It was the very fact of their uselessness that had inspired the idea of the disco. It had seemed like an opportunity to find some real boys from the other years or from outside the school altogether. After all, surely everybody knew some boys, didn't they? And even if they didn't, they weren't going to admit it or even think about it too deeply in the general enthusiasm and excitement. The world was full of boys. They were strewn about the streets, the cafés, they were everywhere. There was almost an epidemic.

39

The disco was at the time a whole month away. Of course one would be able to produce some worthwhile boy by then. And one for a friend, too. Even if there were a mild challenge involved, that made it all the more fun. Of course, the Third Year savages wouldn't be required. It was agreed that no one, absolutely no one, would invite one of *those*.

Annabel was on the committee which had organized the disco, asking for, and obtaining, permission to use the school gym for it. Oh, how heady and exciting it had all been.

As the days advanced and the date of the disco drew nearer, Annabel had begun to wake early in the mornings and shiver. She was facing facts.

She didn't *know* any boys other than those in the Third Year. Not ones that you could show off at the disco, anyway. The battalions of interesting and approachable-looking boys that had previously swarmed everywhere had mysteriously disappeared. Such ones in the other years at Lord Willoughby's who were not positively mis-shapen or malevolent or otherwise disqualified in some way, who had some pretensions to desirability, however feeble, and yet would want to go to the disco, were apparently already booked. There were not very many of them. But apparently there were *some*.

'It's disastrous, Kate,' hissed Annabel now. 'I'm going to be the only one turning up at the disco without a boy. The *only one*.'

Kate was all right. Robert had been able to help her out by providing her with a friend of a friend of his for the evening, one Sigvald, a Norwegian boy who was spending a month in England. Apparently he didn't speak much English but looked quite good and fancied himself at discos, which was more than any of Robert's friends did.

'They're only boasting, Annabel,' Kate said again, feebly. 'They're laying it on.'

'I know, I know. But they wouldn't be able to do that if they hadn't managed to scrape up at least one apiece. *Everybody* seems to have scraped up *something* – except me.'

As if to mock, Julia Channing's voice came floating back to them just before she and Tracey passed out of earshot.

'I think it'll have to be Andrew Torrance. I'm feeling especially guilty about him. He's asked so many times . . .'

She faded out going round the corner and Annabel started.

'Andrew Torrance!' she said, as if in shock. 'She can't have got *him*.'

Andrew Torrance was in the Fifth Year, captain of cricket and winner of this year's Essay Prize. His athleticism and brainpower were matched only by his good looks. He was the pick of the school, certainly in Annabel's eyes. It wouldn't have occurred to her that he might grace their potty disco and even if it had, never in a million years would she have found the nerve to invite him. It wasn't possible that Julia Channing – *Julia Channing* – had landed him. Was it?

In silence, Annabel plucked a dandelion and tore it to pieces. Kate watched sympathetically.

'What am I going to do, Kate?' said Annabel and sighed because she knew there was nothing Kate could usefully say.

'Perhaps you'll find somebody at the fête tomorrow,' said Kate, casting around for anything to say, useful or not.

'At the fête? At Addendon fête? Like who?'

'Oh, I dunno.' It had been a desperate sort of

41

remark. It wasn't fair of Annabel to treat it as if it were a real suggestion. 'Like Barrie Prince, perhaps.'

Barrie Prince was the up and coming young singer who had been invited to open the fête.

'It was only a joke, Annabel.'

Barrie Prince!

A ball, coming from somewhere behind, bounced neatly off the top of Annabel's head and went rolling away ahead of her. Two moronically giggling boys pushed Annabel aside and almost fell on her as they jostled each other in pursuit of it. She had the satisfaction of tripping one up. It proved to be Adrian Webster.

'Sorry, Buncery,' he said as he got to his feet. 'Didn't know it was you.' He dashed off, still giggling inanely.

'Savages!' said Annabel. 'That's the reality. That's the only sort of boy I know. Boys!'

She surveyed the school playing fields. There were boys everywhere. A wealth, a positive mine, of narrow shoulders, tangled hair, vacuous expressions.

'I sometimes wonder what all the fuss is about,' she said.

As if the disco situation weren't bad enough for Annabel's morale, someone was secretly persecuting her. One of the Third Year savages, no doubt. She became convinced of it soon after she had sat down for the first lesson of the afternoon, which was history with Mrs Jesty. She had arrived at the desk first, to be joined by Kate a few moments later.

Still brooding about the disco, it was a minute or two before a feeling of coldness started to penetrate and she realized that she was sitting on something which ought not to be there. Raising herself slightly, she felt to find out what it was and discovered it to be cold and sticky. She half-started out of her seat and looked at her hand to see that it was covered with half-melted choc-ice which had been squeezed out of its wrapping.

Hoping to catch whichever boy had done it in the middle of a triumphant smirk, she looked quickly round. However, not one of them was so much as glancing at her. Nobody was, except for Kate. Everyone else, other than those reading under the desk or daydreaming, was concentrating upon Mrs Jesty, who had just asked a question.

'Yes, Annabel?' she inquired, thinking that Annabel had jumped up eagerly and raised her hand to answer it.

'Marston Moor,' replied Annabel at random, not having heard the question.

'No, no, Annabel, you silly girl. You've got the wrong war,' said Mrs Jesty amiably. 'Do sit down and try to pay attention.'

To tell about the choc-ice would almost certainly rebound. Experience showed that Mrs Jesty would almost certainly become confused and give Annabel a detention for playing the fool in class. Anyway, her skirt was already covered in the stuff. She subsided on to the choc-ice again.

Yes. She had a secret enemy all right. Two days previously, her monogrammed handkerchief given to her for Christmas had disappeared from her desk and a large man's handkerchief, grey with age and with a tear in it, crudely stitched with blue thread, been left in its place.

And now this.

That afternoon, the secret persecutor came out into the open. At least, it might have been him. Afterwards, Annabel wasn't quite sure.

It was while she and Kate were walking home from school along Church Lane. A boy, whom they had noticed following them stealthily on a bicycle, suddenly rode ahead of them and pretended to fall off his bike.

'Oh, my leg, my leg!' he groaned, writhing in the gutter and clasping his right leg. 'I've hurt it. Help me. Help me.'

'He thinks we're stupid,' said Annabel.

Clearly, in her opinion, he only wanted to entice them close to him before producing a water-pistol or some other weapon.

'You're sure it's not real?' said Kate, a little doubtfully. 'He doesn't look like a practical joker, does he?'

He didn't. He was small and squat. His trousers were too short for him and his blazer was too long. His mousey hair, which stuck up at the crown, fell forward in a pudding-basin fringe over his low forehead, blinking eyes and pale, puddingy face, which was at the moment screwed up in a semblance of suffering.

'I expect he's compensating,' said Annabel. 'The psychiatrists would explain it.'

She stooped and picked up a stone, then pretended to throw it with all her might.

The agonized expression on the boy's face was instantly replaced by one of genuine alarm and he leapt to his feet. He scrambled quickly back on to his bike and pedalled off round the bend.

'I don't think he can be my secret persecutor, though,' said Annabel, dropping the stone. 'I don't even know his name. He's in the Second Year, isn't he? I've seen him about, that's all.'

'I remember now,' said Kate. 'His name's Matthew Parkin – or is it Parkin Matthew? I'm not sure which. I only know that because when he was in the First

Year he won the Da Susa award for Best Trier of the Year. Remember?'

'Oh, yes,' said Annabel. 'Now you mention it . . .' Her expression softened a little. 'Then life hasn't been all that easy for him, has it?'

The award had been a short-lived affair, having only been presented for the one year. Although Mrs da Susa didn't normally approve of prizes she had decided a couple of years previously that there was a case for presenting one to the worst, most hopeless dud of the First Year on the grounds that it would give him or her some small but necessary moment of glory and perhaps purpose in life.

She had therefore, after much thought, selected a title for the award, added her own name to it and chosen Parkin Matthew – or was it Matthew Parkin? – as its first recipient. Overcome with confusion and embarrassment while being presented with it on Speech Day, he had stumbled while climbing the steps to the platform, fallen against the table on which all the proper trophies and prizes were assembled, almost knocking them over, and banged his head. This had caused his eyes to water so much that he had had to be helped off the platform with his prize by a sympathetic Mrs da Susa.

Instead of the hoped-for glory and spur to effort, the prize had brought him nothing but derision and almost destroyed his morale altogether since it was quite obvious to the meanest intelligence, including his own, why Mrs da Susa had selected him for it. Other pupils of Lord Willoughby's had run after him in the streets calling out the name of his award, not in the tones of admiration for which Mrs da Susa would have hoped, but disrespectfully and mockingly.

Mrs da Susa, perhaps dimly realizing that things had not gone strictly according to plan, had somehow forgotten about the award by the time next Speech Day had come round and it seemed unlikely that it would be revived. Parkin Matthew might well, therefore, occupy a small niche in history as its only holder. It was, too, perhaps the only award he would ever win, which was just as well since any further similar ones might have ruined his life altogether.

This, then, was the reason for the look of sympathy which crossed Annabel's face. But her mind soon reverted to her own troubles, which were great.

'I don't think he could be my secret persecutor,' she said, frowning, 'unless ... oh, Kate – do you think he's just one of them? Maybe all the boys are persecuting me –'

'Oh, Annabel –'

'Do you think they all dislike me, Kate? Am I a total, utter failure?'

'*Annabel!*'

'With boys I'm just a non-achiever.'

In vain did Kate try to comfort her and make her realise how popular she was. But then, wasn't her dejection just a little understandable? To be persecuted by the winner of the Da Susa Best Trier Award ... !

'Oh, Kate! What hope is there for me when I've sunk as low as this?'

Yet the next day was to see the beginning of a remarkable change in Annabel's fortunes. It happened at the fête.

For quite a number of pupils at Lord Willoughby's, the chief attraction of the fête was that it gave an opportunity to see Barrie Prince in person.

Barrie Prince, whose real name was Barry Krinks, had lived fairly locally, about a dozen miles from Addendon, until acquiring mild fame as a minor star of the provincial stage with the occasional appearance on television. His talent, for muttering soulful and romantic songs into a microphone, while accompanying himself on the piano, had emerged early. He had started appearing at local concerts when he was twelve and he was now still only seventeen. It was assumed by everyone that everything he had achieved so far was merely a beginning and that a brilliant future lay ahead of him.

Annabel wasn't particularly conscious of this. Musically, she regarded herself as a classicist. She played second violin in the school orchestra under Mr Polegate and also dabbled with the clarinet.

Kate, too, played in the school orchestra, mainly to humour Annabel. Her instrument was the recorder.

Neither of them, therefore, was a particular fan of Barrie Prince and it was mainly curiosity that prompted them to get to the fête early enough to join the admiring throng that surrounded him as he made the opening speech. Behind him, a semicircle of town dignitaries jostled each other, trying to catch a little reflected glory.

Kate noticed Julia Channing clasping and unclasping her hands ecstatically. 'I've met him before,' she was boasting. 'We had a chat and he gave me his autograph.'

Justine Bird was standing just in front of her, accompanied by a youth with an elaborate hair style and wearing a leather jacket, one of her 'fellers'. She turned her head and looked Julia Channing up and down, wearily closing and opening her blackly mascara-ed eyes. Then she let her face loll moronically and suddenly expelled a huge bubble of bubble-gum into the startled Julia's face. Retrieving it, she returned her attention to Barrie Prince.

'That was quite neatly done,' said Kate, admiringly. She hadn't realized that Justine had such powers of expression. They had never been evident in English.

Annabel wasn't listening.

'Gosh!' she said.

She was staring in fascination at Barrie Prince.

'He's reminded me of what boys are all about,' she said. 'The Third Year lot had got me confused – but him – yes, there is a point to them, after all.'

He was a lesson to all Third Year savages, an example for them to aim at, however hopelessly. He was tall and slender with a pale, sensitive face, brown spaniel eyes and dark, crisp, curly hair. He was at present engaged in making some sort of speech of welcome. It was totally inaudible because of the size of the crowd that surrounded him but that didn't matter. Kate noticed that Annabel's mouth had fallen open.

The speech seemed to be over. Barrie Prince was smiling and raising his hands and his audience was applauding and otherwise signifying its approval. Annabel heaved a sudden sigh and turned away.

'I've just been having a little day-dream, Kate,' she said. 'I was dreaming that I was turning up at the Third Year disco with Barrie Prince in tow. I was imagining the look on Julia's face – and Tracey's.'

She sighed again and closed her eyes for a moment.

'Never mind,' she said. 'Let's have a look at the fête.'

Annabel spent most of her money very quickly. This was chiefly because she fell in love with one of the prizes at the hoop-la stall – a bracelet – and became obsessed with winning it. It was futile for Kate to remind her that she could probably buy a similar one very cheaply in a shop. Apparently crazed with desire for it, Annabel had go after go, but in vain. Suddenly she forgot all about it again.

'I've still got enough for a go on the swing-boats,' she said. 'Come on, Kate – treat you.'

Kate didn't want to be treated.

'I don't like swing-boats,' she said – but Annabel was already on her way. Annabel *did* like swing-boats and, after all, it wasn't a pleasure she was able to indulge in very often. The least a friend could do was not to grouse. So Kate sighed and joined her in a swing-boat.

It was only when they were starting to swing high that Kate remembered exactly *why* she disliked them.

'Annabel,' she said, 'I'm beginning to feel a bit sick.'

'What?' said Annabel, giving another pull on the rope. 'Look, Kate, there's Barrie Prince.'

Barrie Prince, followed by a retinue of fawning dignitaries and a trail of fans, was making a tour of the fête with a smile and a wave here, a little word there. He had just had a go on the rifle range and was turning to make his way past the swing-boats. The rapt expression reappeared on Annabel's face.

'I said I feel sick,' called Kate, from somewhere above Barrie Prince's head. He heard her, for he flinched and the smile faded slightly, then he looked up at her.

'Eh? Oh! Better get off then,' said Annabel, returning to reality with a start.

She stopped pulling. The next they knew, Barrie Prince was seizing the swing-boat and hauling on it to slow it down.

'Can't have you feeling sick,' said he, gallantly, and held a hand out to the startled Kate to help her down. Then he looked at Annabel.

'And we can't have you left by yourself, can we?' he said. And before Annabel could quite realize what was happening he was hauling himself up to take Kate's place in the swing-boat opposite her.

'Come on,' he said. *'Swing!'*

They pulled on their ropes in harmony and swung together into a finer, golden world. Annabel saw only the swaying vision of dark, curly hair and soulful eyes as he smiled at her. All else had vanished, the watching dignitaries and fans, the photographer from the *Addendon Weekly Advertiser* taking his pictures. The swing-boat was the universe.

Higher and higher they soared and Annabel's heart went lifting into the clouds. And now, to cap it all, he was singing to her. In that low, yet carrying, husky mutter, to the tune of the Eton Boating Song, he sang . . .

> 'Swing, swing together,
> Higher and higher we go,
> Pull on our ropes together,
> Give 'em a real good show . . .'

Lyrics composed and sung for her alone. For no other . . .

And, watching awe-stricken from below as they soared first to one side then the other, Kate heard Annabel's voice raised in chorus with his. They were singing together as well as swinging, to each other and to the clouds, their voices soaring remotely as the swing-boat reached the end of its travel to left or right, then becoming momentarily loud as they flashed close by.

> 'Then swing, swing together
> And give 'em a re-heal good show-ho-ho-ho.'

It was subsiding, stopping. Barrie Prince was helping Annabel out. The *Advertiser*'s camera flashed yet again.

'Pity I've got another appointment,' he was saying, still holding her hand. 'I'd have liked to stay in that swing-boat a lot longer.'

'For always,' said Annabel, who was still in an enchanted world.

'What's your name?' he asked. He still hadn't let go of her hand and the *Advertiser* was taking yet another picture.

'Annabel Fidelity Bunce.'

'Might see you around,' he said. 'I'm staying in the area for a week or two.'

Then abruptly he turned away, to be seized upon by the dignitaries.

'Like – like a Prince who's managed to escape his courtiers for a few precious minutes!' said Annabel. He was being escorted away, turning out of sight behind the guess-the-weight-of-the-cake stall. 'Kate, do you think I made an impression on him? Do you think –?'

'What?' said Kate.

'Why did he ask my name?'

Without waiting for a reply, Annabel suddenly started after him, hoping to catch one last glimpse of him before he disappeared.

Someone was barring her way, however. A boy. Parkin Matthew. As she tried to dodge past him he made to stop her with his left hand. He was holding his right one behind his back, hiding something. He obviously had some sort of weapon there –

'Got something for you –' he was leering.

'Please stop persecuting me,' said Annabel. She was at least half a head taller than he was. Before he could do anything, she gave him a firm push which sent him sprawling backwards to sit down in a muddy patch. Then, followed by Kate, she ran.

But Barrie Prince was driving off in a big, flash, yellow car, waved away by the dignitaries.

'Why did he ask me for my name, Kate?' said Annabel, for the umpteenth time in minutes. 'Why did he say he might see me around? Now *why*?'

'I don't know, Annabel,' said Kate, yet again.

'I'll have my picture in the *Advertiser* – with him. I can't wait till next Friday.'

The *Advertiser* appeared on Fridays.

'Which picture do you think they'll choose? The one in the swing-boat? Helping me out? Holding my hand as we parted?'

'Perhaps they'll make a spread of them all.'

'Do you think so? Do you really think so?'

Annabel glowed.

'But why did he ask my name, Kate? And what did he mean when he said he might see me around?'

'I don't know, Annabel.'

They were looking around the fête for other girls from 3G. It was troubling Annabel slightly that although there were several at the fête, not one of them had come up to her to discuss Barrie Prince. At least one or two of them must have seen him in the swing-boat with her or, at any rate, had heard about it. So why weren't they saying anything about it? Envy, presumably. That malignant serpent, envy.

Julia Channing and Tracey Cooke were at the roll-a-penny stall. Justine Bird, with her feller beside her, was watching them, impassively chewing, leaning against the stall with one elbow resting on her feller's shoulder.

'I've just been in the swing-boats with Barrie Prince,' said Annabel, carelessly, joining Julia and Tracey.

52

'Yes, we saw,' said Tracey, equally carelessly. She rolled her coin.

There was a silence.

'Bad luck!' said Julia. 'I'll have a go.'

Justine's feller nudged her and jerked his hand and they drifted away.

'He went on just about everything,' said Tracey. 'Good for publicity, I suppose. It gets his name in the papers.'

'We had our picture taken together,' said Annabel.

'Yes,' said Julia. 'They were taking his picture everywhere. Oh dear! That's all my money gone.'

'Come on, Kate,' said Annabel. 'We might as well go.'

Walking home, her face quivered.

'They're right, aren't they, Kate? He didn't mean anything. I expect he was just putting it all on for the photographer . . .

'I'd been having my day-dreams again – about going to the disco with him. You can laugh if you want to, Kate. I wouldn't blame you . . .

'I can't find *anybody* to go to the disco with me. All the boys do is persecute me. And yet there was I day-dreaming about Barrie Prince. It's funny, isn't it, really funny . . .' From somewhere in her throat came a little moan. 'Oh, Kate, what am I going to do?'

But next morning the message arrived. It was in a sealed, perfumed envelope, with ANNABEL BUNCE neatly handwritten in capitals on it, and must have been delivered during the night for Annabel's mother found it lying on the mat when she got up in the morning.

It was quite sensational. It was all written in capitals and read:

53

DEAR ANNABEL,

I KNOW THAT IT IS CRAZY TO WRITE TO YOU
BUT I CANNOT GO ON LIKE THIS. EVER SINCE
WHAT PASSED BETWEEN US AT THE FETE I
HAVE BEEN TORCHERING MYSELF BECAUSE I
KNOW THERE CAN BE NOTHING BETWEEN US.

PERHAPS YOU CAN GUESS WHO I AM,
THOUGH PERHAPS IT WOULD BE BETTER IF
YOU CAN'T, BUT ANYWAY I CAN ONLY WORSHIP
YOU FROM AFAR.

I WRITE THIS NOTE TO ASK YOU A FAVOUR.
WILL YOU WRITE TO ME SOMETIMES? PLEASE
FORGET WHO I MIGHT BE. THINK OF ME AS
THE BOY YOU SEE IN YOUR IMAGINATION
WHEN YOU'RE TRYING TO THINK OF
SOMEBODY MARVELLUS. SINCE I CAN'T TELL
YOU MY REAL NAME, CALL ME 'GAVIN'.

IF YOU WILL ONLY DO THIS YOU WILL EASE
THE PAIN IN MY HEART. LET ME KNOW BY
GIVING ME A SIGN. LEAVE YOUR FAVOURITE
FLOWER UNDER THE SEAT NEAR THE SWINGS
IN ADDENDON REC. THERE'S A PIECE OF
BROKEN DRAINPIPE UNDER THERE WHICH
COULD BE OUR LETTER-BOX.

I LONG TO HEAR FROM YOU. DO NOT BREAK
MY HEART.

                    YOUR DEVOTED SLAVE
                    GAVIN

P.S. I SAY A FLOWER BECAUSE I THINK OF YOU
AS MY FAIR FLOWER.

'He sounds cracked,' said Kate, when Annabel
showed her the message later that morning. 'Spell-
ing's a bit weak as well. You're sure it's not a
joke?'

54

'Why does it have to be a joke?' asked Annabel, indignantly. 'Or cracked?'

'Oh, no reason,' said Kate, with hasty diplomacy. Anyway, Annabel was right. Why did it? Why did she never get messages like that?

'His fair flower,' said Annabel, lingering lovingly over each word. 'Torturing himself over me . . .' She gave a delicious little squirm. 'His devoted slave . . . perhaps there's some light at the end of the tunnel, Kate.'

'What does that mean?' asked Kate.

'You're not asking me who I think it is, Kate. Who do *you* think?'

'Well, I –'

'Pretty obvious, isn't it. Couldn't make it clearer without actually saying so. All those hints –'

'I suppose –'

'What passed between us at the fête yesterday . . . having to keep his identity secret . . . Kate, it's all unbelievable, isn't it, but it *must* be him.'

'Barrie Prince?'

'Who else?' Annabel's spirits were sky-high this morning.

'But how would he find your address?'

'Phone book, of course.'

'But – why couldn't there be anything between you – I mean, why would he have to keep his identity secret?'

'Oh, I can see that. His career . . .' Annabel gave another little squirm of pleasure – 'all those gossip columnists. I mean, that's what makes it so certain it's him, Kate. Who else would have to keep his identity secret?'

'It is fantastic, isn't it?' said Kate. 'But – well, yes, I don't see who else it could be. Are you going to leave him his flower?'

'Course I am,' said Annabel. She sighed and her voice became wistful. 'A secret romance by letter with – with *Gavin* – oh, Kate, isn't it beautiful?' Then her voice became more practical. 'Things are looking up, aren't they?'

The flower was a garden daisy. With it was a piece of straw. Annabel had to wait until two elderly ladies had vacated the seat before going to the drainpipe because, as she said, they might think it was a bit funny.

'What's the straw for?' Kate wanted to know.

'It's the language of flowers. I got it out of a book. The garden daisy means "I share your sentiments" and the piece of unbroken straw means agreement. I thought it's a touch he might like. He's obviously very romantic.'

'But do you think he'll know what they mean? Supposing he just thinks it's a piece of straw?'

'If he doesn't, it's just too bad. He's got my note, anyway.'

To go with the daisy and straw, Annabel had written a little note which she put in an envelope addressed to 'Gavin'. It read:

Dear Gavin,
Thank you for your letter. I should very much like to have a correspondence with you.
Looking forward to hearing from you again soon and please don't torture yourself too much.

Yours,
Annabel Bunce

'What are you going to write about?' said Kate, as they left the recreation ground. 'I mean, it's not going

56

to be easy, is it, when you're not even supposed to know who you're writing to.'

'You haven't got any romance, Kate,' said Annabel, blandly. Then she added, rather mysteriously – 'Anyway, I know what *I'm* going to write about.'

Annabel was her old cheerful self again at school next day. In fact she was positively burbling. It didn't go unnoticed.

'You're looking very happy today,' Julia Channing observed while everyone was eating their sandwiches during the lunch break. She eyed Annabel narrowly. 'You've seemed a bit worried lately, if you don't mind my saying so.'

'Oh, I have been worried,' said Annabel, taking an apple from her box. 'Yes, it's been a very worrying time for me really, trying to decide who to bring to the disco. But I think I've made my decision now.'

She bit into the apple and complacently watched Julia Channing shift uncomfortably about in her seat.

'Er – who'd that be?' enquired Tracey, trying to look off-hand.

'You'll see,' said Annabel.

'Anybody we know?' Julia asked, casually.

'Yes, yes, in a way I suppose you do,' said Annabel. 'Come on, Kate. Let's go outside.'

She almost gave a little skip as they went out of the door. The Channing offensive had been halted in its tracks. Soon it would be time to get her on the run.

Annabel's self-confidence was due to the fact that she had already had another message from Gavin. It had been waiting for her in the drainpipe, which she had peeped into on her way to school that morning, without any real hope that anything would be there so soon.

MY BEAUTIFUL ANNABEL
I AM SO STUNNED WITH JOY THAT I CAN'T
THINK WHAT TO WRITE ABOUT JUST FOR
NOW. BUT I SHALL. YOU ARE CLEOPATRA
AND I AM YOUR JULIUS SEESAR. YOU ARE
GWINEVERE AND I SIR LANSELOT, YOUR
NIGHT OF THE ROUND TABLE. GIVE ME A
QUEST SO THAT I CAN SHOW MY DEVOTION.
ACTIONS ARE BETTER THAN WORDS.
ANYTHING THAT'S WITHIN MY POWER I'LL
DO FOR YOU. I WAIT YOUR COMMAND.

                    TILL ETERNITY
                    GAVIN

Enclosed in the envelope had been an aromatic leaf
which Annabel had identified as a bay leaf. According
to her book, which she was keeping in her schoolbag,
it meant 'I change but in death'. So Gavin knew about
the language of flowers.

Annabel had leapt for joy. 'Anything within his
power! He awaits my command!' she had cried,
showing it to Kate. She had written a reply on the
spot:

Dear Gavin,
It's lovely of you to offer. There's one thing I'd
like more than anything else. I'd like you to
come to the Lord Willoughby's Third Year disco
with me. It's on Saturday at 7 o'clock.

                    Yours,
                    Annabel

Annabel was trying to flush Gavin out. And quickly. A purely literary Gavin, though flattering, was of
little practical use. She needed his solid presence.

'He won't come,' said Kate now. 'Why should he?
He wants to keep his identity secret.'

But Annabel seemed sublimely confident. She wasn't even bothering to argue.

'Perhaps, Kate,' she said, 'perhaps this romance will blossom and grow. It's early days yet but one day maybe . . .'

'Mrs Prince?' suggested Kate.

Annabel simpered.

'Who knows what the future might hold?' she said, coyly blushing.

As Kate had anticipated, Gavin's next note showed signs of alarm.

MY OWN SWEETHEART, (it read.) YOU ASK ME
THE ONE THING I CANNOT DO. WE CAN
NEVER MEET. YOU MUST NEVER KNOW MY
TRUE IDENTITY. PLEASE FIND A DIFFERENT
QUEST.

There followed more endearments and enclosed with the note was a sprig of ivy, which was found to mean 'assiduous to please'.

Annabel replied promptly. Time was of the essence. Deciding that her previous messages had been dull in comparison with Gavin's she ventured into a slightly more imaginative and persuasive style.

Dearest Heart,
I haven't got any other quests and besides, I long
for you to come to the disco with me. You see,
dear heart, *I know your secret*. I KNOW who
you are. Oh, dear heart, let us meet openly just
for this one time at least. Could anything be
more romantic? We'll meet beneath the conker
tree at the corner of Church Lane and Apsley
Road at ten to seven and then walk together
into the disco hand in hand. It will be one

beautiful evening to remember always. Dear
heart, you have nothing to lose.

                                    Yours,
                                    Annabel

There was what could only have been a stunned
silence from Gavin. No message came the next day or
the day after that. By Friday, Annabel's confidence
was faltering slightly. She was on edge. But so,
thought Kate, were several other of the 3G girls.
There was a general air of tension about.

'This – er – this boy you're bringing to the disco,'
said Julia Channing at lunch time. 'He's still coming,
is he?'

'Just try and keep him away!' laughed Annabel,
gaily.

Julia's face twitched and then a look of intense
gloom settled over it. She was clearly in dread of
being out-gunned.

Kate herself was able to stand aside from all this
emotion. On the previous evening Robert had introduced her to Sigvald. She had vaguely thought all
Norwegians to be tall and fair but he had turned out
to be short and dark, with warts. He had pointed at
her, said 'Disco! Hah', given her a thumbs-up sign,
then placed one hand on his hip and started shrugging
his shoulders in a studiedly careless sort of way.
Robert had looked on with indulgent contempt as if
to say 'You wanted an idiot – see, I've found you a
prize one.'

Perhaps she didn't have Annabel's heady excite-
ments. But then she didn't have the worries either.

Annabel and Kate looked in at the recreation
ground on the way home from school but there
was still no message in the drainpipe. Annabel was
anxious but not giving up hope.

Too impatient to wait for the *Advertiser* to be

delivered, she persuaded Kate to accompany her to the newsagents to look at it there. It was disappointing. There was a picture of Barrie Prince at the fête but it showed him embracing Justine Bird with one arm while using the other to hurl a coconut. Justine was accepting his embrace as if it were her due while nonchalantly chatting to her feller who stood on the other side of her.

'That must have been before he met me,' said Annabel, with an attempt at taking it graciously. But she wasn't pleased.

And then, coming out of the newsagents, Annabel gave a sudden shriek.

'It's him,' she cried.

A flash yellow car was just passing, its driver crouched at the wheel, intent on working his way to the front of a stream of other cars.

'Gavin!' Annabel shrieked on sudden impulse. She started waving and jumping up and down on the pavement.

Kate saw clearly the startled face of Barrie Prince as he turned his head and braked hard, causing the driver behind to do the same. He appeared to be about to stop, then was forced onwards by the hooting and flashing from behind. He disappeared round the bend in the High Street.

'That showed him,' cried Annabel. 'That showed him I *know*. Oh, Kate – it's fate, isn't it, bumping into him like this. He'll come. Now I know he'll come.'

And as if that weren't enough, another sign came that evening. Annabel was so moved by it that she rang up Kate straight away to tell her. Apparently her father had asked her to turn on the radio for the news and when she had switched it on she had immediately heard – guess what? – Barrie Prince singing!

She had only been able to listen for a few moments

because her father had told her that wasn't the news and to switch that racket off. She had heard only one line of his song but that line was fantastic. It had been –

I'll come to you.

And next morning Annabel arrived breathlessly on Kate's doorstep. The message had arrived. It was majestic in its simplicity.

BE WAITING. I SHALL COME – GAVIN

At about twenty past six that evening Kate, attired for the disco in denim dungarees, called for Annabel.

Her own meeting, with Sigvald, wasn't till seven o'clock or perhaps a little later. Sigvald had intimated through Robert that he would simply turn up at the disco without any prior formalities – so Kate had agreed to keep Annabel company as far as the conker tree.

It was some time before there was any response to her ring at the bell. Then the door opened a crack and an eye peered out.

'Oh, it's you,' said Annabel. 'Thank goodness!' To Kate's surprise there was a tremor in her voice.

'Who did you think it was?' asked Kate.

'It could have been Mum and Dad. They went out. They might have forgotten something.' She pulled the door open wide.

'Annabel!' said Kate, startled.

She was wearing a dress which Kate took to be someone else's, someone who wasn't quite her height and shape. It was a lurid purple colour and was cut a little off-the-shoulder, revealing her freckles.

Kate's eyes travelled upwards towards Annabel's face. There was something seriously wrong there.

'Somebody's given you a black eye,' she said, indignantly.

'It's eye shadow,' said Annabel. 'I was just going to do the other one when you rang the bell. Come on. Somebody might see me.'

Annabel's face was altogether extraordinary. The black of the eye shaded irregularly into pallid cheeks, which turned to an unusual shade of pale mauve at the lips. She looked like a clown in lurid lighting.

'Where'd you get all this stuff from?' asked Kate, when they were upstairs in Annabel's room.

'Justine Bird. I went round to see her this afternoon. This dress is her mother's. Do you know, Kate – Justine borrows her mother's things all the time. They're the same size, or nearly the same size, anyway.'

Annabel sat down in front of the mirror and started dabbing at the other eye. Kate noticed that her hand appeared to be shaking.

'Justine's not bad when you get to know her. Hasn't got a lot to say but she's very helpful. Look, she lent me some fashion shoes as well.'

Annabel indicated a pair of pink, high-heeled shoes beneath her dressing-table.

'I mean all I've got are my school lace-ups and a pair of trainers and the toes are nearly through from kicking stones about –'

Annabel was babbling nervously and relentlessly.

'But Annabel,' Kate cut in, gently. 'I'm going in my old dungarees and plimsolls. I should think most people'll be in much the same sort of thing.'

'Yes, I know, Kate, but –' Annabel was obviously trying to put it as kindly as she could – 'you're not going with Barrie Prince, are you? You haven't got to meet him after all the build-up in those notes, have you . . .'

She was suddenly convulsed by a shudder and the mascara stick dropped from her fingers and fell to the floor. She started to pick it up but instead, giving a dramatic groan, she fell forward on to the dressing table, burying her face in her arms.

'Kate, I'm terrified. I've actually got to meet him – talk to him – in not much more than a quarter of an hour. What do I say to him –?'

Kate understood and sympathized. Annabel had come down to earth. Barrie Prince had at last taken shape in her mind as a real, solid human being instead of being a shining pink cloud in the sky.

'But, Annabel, it doesn't help to dress up like that –'

'I've got to. He's sophisticated, Kate, a man of the world, famous. I've got to try and look sophisticated as well. If I don't make myself look older he'll – he'll think he's just got a spotty schoolgirl –'

'But you are a –' began Kate, then stopped. There wasn't any point.

It started to rain as they walked towards the school, gently at first then more heavily. For Kate, it made the expedition even less enjoyable than it already was. Escorting Annabel to her rendezvous with destiny was much like escorting a querulous and infirm old lady to a dental appointment.

The shoes, which had seemed reasonably well fitting when Annabel first put them on, very quickly began to pinch at the toes while slopping at the heels so that she began to hobble along in a feet-dragging crouch, muttering to herself. The hobble was accentuated because the skirt of Mrs Bird's dress was tight and Annabel was not used to tight skirts.

'If it weren't that I've got a picture of Julia's face in my mind,' said Annabel, morosely, 'I think I'd go home now.'

Kate noticed that the mascara was running slightly as the rain got at it. She started to say something about it then decided not to. What was the point of demoralizing Annabel still further?

They came in sight of the conker tree with a minute or two to spare. There was no one there. Heavy drops of rain were dripping from the branches and it didn't look as romantic as it usually did. It looked, in fact, uninviting.

'We could stand in the bus shelter until you see him turn up,' Kate suggested. 'Better than just getting more wet.'

Annabel seemed incapable of speaking by now but she nodded and they turned into the bus shelter. From there, they would be able to keep watch on the conker tree. Presumably Barry Prince would turn up in his flash car.

There was someone already in the bus shelter, a short, squat boy, his back towards them, looking an absolute twit in a dark grey suit with razor-edge creases and a white collar that climbed high up the back of his neck almost, it seemed, to where his hair stood up on end at the crown. He was holding a bunch of flowers and staring along Church Lane. He didn't even look round as they entered, merely stepped a little further along and went on staring.

Annabel was shivering, whether from fear, or the cold, Kate couldn't quite tell. Several minutes passed by and, but for the sound of the rain beating with steady severity on the roof of the bus shelter, there was silence.

Kate looked at her watch. It was three minutes to seven. Since there was nothing she could usefully say, she glanced again at the boy who was sharing the shelter with them. There was something familiar about that hair-style, that thick neck and squat back.

Annabel leaned across and tapped the boy on the shoulder.

'Excuse me,' she said, 'but you haven't noticed a big yellow car passing by, have you?'

'No,' said the boy, turning to look at them for the first time. 'I'm waiting –'

He stopped speaking and recoiled slightly as he got a good view of Annabel. She was an unexpected sight to come across in an Addendon bus shelter on a wet Saturday evening.

'Parkin Matthew!' exclaimed Annabel, astonished.

It was her persecutor. He peered at her, mouth open. 'Matthew Parkin,' he corrected her, indignantly but mechanically. He couldn't seem to believe his eyes.

'What are you doing here?' Annabel asked him, crossly. 'Why do you keep on popping up everywhere –'

She paused. She had noticed that there was a card hanging from the bunch of flowers he was holding and it seemed to her that she had caught a glimpse of a familiar name written upon it in large block capitals. She took the card between her fingers. On it were the words:

TO MY SWEETHEART,
FROM GAVIN

'Gavin!' she said, blankly.

'You – you really are Annabel, then,' he said. 'I recognize your voice now.'

'Then – *you're* Gavin! You've been standing here waiting for *me*!'

With a groan, Annabel tottered to the seat and sat down. He looked at her.

'But you thought I was somebody else,' he said, 'Somebody in a yellow car.' He, too, sank down on the seat. His nose twitched and his hair, which had somehow been held back, perhaps by water which had now dried, slid forward into its accustomed fringe again. 'I should have known better than to believe you when you said you knew who I was. I should have known it was a mistake.'

'But, I mean,' said Annabel, desperately trying to adjust her mind, 'why should I have thought it was you? You were persecuting me. When you fell off your bike –'

'I wasn't persecuting you. I was just trying to get to know you. Nothing else had worked.'

'Did – did you leave a choc-ice on my seat?'

'It was a present. I know you like choc-ices. I've seen you buying them.'

'Was it you that pinched my handkerchief?'

'I wanted a keepsake. I knew I shouldn't have done it but I did leave you a bigger one in its place. I carry it around everywhere.'

'But – but – that day at the fête – when you tried to stop me. You had something behind your back.'

'It was this,' he said, producing something from his pocket. 'I won it for you at the hoop-la. I knew you wanted it so I just stayed there till I won it. I've brought it for you now.'

He handed it to her. It was the bracelet she had craved. She had forgotten all about it.

Then he looked at the bunch of flowers.

'Sweet peas,' he said. 'They mean "delicate plea-sures".' He tossed them on to the seat, rose and started to mooch away, hands in his pockets.

'But how *could* I know it was you?' cried Annabel. 'You said in your note something about what passed between us at the fête. *What* passed between us at the fête?'

'You pushed me into the mud,' he said, without pausing.

It was only then that Annabel seemed fully to

realize what had happened. She was being left alone. With a choice of having to go to the disco either alone or with Matthew Parkin, even Matthew Parkin seemed preferable. She jumped to her feet.

'Wait,' she said. 'Perhaps we can rescue something. Perhaps –'

He was just outside the shelter, in the rain. He turned and looked at her. It was probably the one dignified moment of his life.

'I don't want to rescue anything,' he said. 'You look terrible. I'd be ashamed to be seen with you at a disco. Anyway, you can't even get my name the right way round.'

About to turn away again, he paused, took the bracelet from her hand and put it in his pocket.

'Cost me all my pocket money, that did,' he said bitterly. 'Here, you might as well have your handkerchief back, though.'

He walked off, going round the back of the shelter, where he could be heard moving around. He must have parked his bike round there.

Annabel sat down again, head bowed, hands clasped on her lap. She appeared to be shuddering.

'Rejected by Par – by Matthew Parkin,' she muttered. 'Rejected by the winner of the Da Susa Best Trier Award. It's the ultimate humiliation, isn't it, Kate?'

She brushed her eyes with the handkerchief which Matthew Parkin had returned to her, causing the mascara to smear right across her face. Kate patted her shoulder sympathetically.

'And no more than I deserve!' Annabel said suddenly and defiantly. She jumped to her feet and ran out of the bus shelter.

Now wearing a yellow cycling cape, Matthew Parkin was wobbling away on his bicycle.

'Matthew!' she yelled. 'Gavin! I think ours was a beautiful relationship. I was dazzled by false glamour but I'm sorry now.'

However, Matthew Parkin did not look round.

It was some twenty minutes later that Kate led Annabel into the disco. In that time she had got her back home, washed and into her own clothes again.

She almost had to be dragged inside. Kate herself wasn't looking forward to it because she was very late and was worried about having kept Sigvald waiting.

However, she need not have been. Sigvald wasn't there. He had, presumably, forgotten about it. Andrew Torrance wasn't there, either. In fact the only outsider who had turned up was a pale-faced youth with a cloud of frizzy ginger hair, another of Justine's fellers. They were dancing together, with casual expertise, in the centre of the gym, which had been transformed for the evening into a pulsing, flickering cavern.

Otherwise the only boys present were from the Third Year at Lord Willoughby's. They were all shuffling and shambling about together in a circle at one end of the cavern, presumably under the illusion that they were dancing. Mr Ribbons was amongst them.

At the other end of the cavern another similar shambling circle revealed itself, when the eyes had become accustomed to the gloom and the flickerings, to be composed of the Third Year girls. Julia, who was amongst them, had clearly been watching the door for she waved at Annabel and Kate as they came in. Her relief at seeing Annabel without a partner was manifest.

''Lo, Annabel. 'Lo, Kate,' she was shrieking. 'Lovely, isn't it. Most of the boys have come. Nice to see so many, isn't it?'

Some of the boys looked round and waved and shouted too, for of course Annabel had always been very popular. They really were rather a nice crowd.

Annabel, peacemaker

*****

There was a period, unfortunately brief, when Annabel's prestige stood very high with Kate's family. She became indeed something of a heroine to all the residents of Oakwood Crescent, the street in which Kate lived.

This was because of the – apparently – brilliant way in which she dealt with a problem which had defeated them all: how to get rid of the gangs of boys who used to fight on the Green outside their houses every evening. Where they had tried threats and abuse and failed, Annabel – apparently – had used subtlety and succeeded.

Though the true facts were not *quite* like that . . .

It had started with the long summer evenings. A crowd of boys, mostly about eight or nine years old and in two rival gangs, began having nightly battles, pummelling and wresting with each other and making the most intolerable din with their yells and war-cries.

There didn't seem to be anything vicious about it; they had all the appearance of enjoying themselves. But the residents of Oakwood Crescent had to keep their windows closed against the noise and could still have difficulty in hearing themselves speak.

'Why can't they sit at home and watch telly like everybody else?' Kate's father would snarl. 'It's like a slum round here with them outside.' Like other parents living immediately around the Green, he had made the occasional sortie to shout threats at the boys and try to get rid of them but with no success. They might scatter for a little while but would return with joyous shrieks the moment his back was turned.

Even Kate, who wasn't normally averse to noise, found it a bit much and she said so to Annabel one evening. Annabel had called for her and they were on their way to a meeting at the Church Hall. The boys were on the Green, as usual, fighting and yelling.

Annabel was, however, unsympathetic.

'Honestly, Kate!' she shouted primly above the racket. 'I'm amazed to find you such a spoilsport. I think it's a relief to see them out here in the fresh air. So many boys just sit and blink at television all the time, something I'm feeling very strongly about just now.'

'Yes, I suppose so,' said Kate, a little doubtfully, 'but –'

'Anyway, don't you realize that all healthy boys of that age *must* fight. They enjoy it. It's part of their nature.'

Kate shut up and they walked the rest of the way to the Church Hall in silence. Annabel seemed broody and preoccupied.

They weren't many people in the Church Hall but that wasn't surprising. The meeting had been organized by Mrs Stringer, a fat busybody who was a leading member of the Addendon Town Council. She lived in hopes of being elected Mayor and sought to keep herself in the public eye by constantly arranging public meetings on any and every subject, usually with visiting speakers.

Annabel and Kate attended many of the meetings for the sake of the refreshments, which were free and invariably lavish and excellent. Whatever her other shortcomings, Mrs Stringer had an eye for that sort of detail. It didn't seem to bother her, or probably she was too self-important to notice, that, like Annabel and Kate, most of the people who came along were only there for the free tea. About half were still at school, some from Lord Willoughby's, some still at primary.

The visiting speaker on this occasion was the Deputy Director of an organization dedicated to international peace and understanding and he spoke for about twenty minutes on the subject. Normally, Annabel and Kate would have spent much of the time whispering together but on this occasion Annabel still seemed preoccupied. She sat gazing at the speaker, a frown on her face, and refused to be distracted.

When he'd finished, Mrs Stringer got up, ostensibly to thank him and ask for questions. Once on her feet, however, she virtually forgot about him, obviously feeling that he'd hogged the floor long enough, and launched into a speech of her own, using what he had said as a peg. His talk about international understanding had been a bit over her head, being too global and abstract, and she sought to reduce it to terms which she and perhaps her audience would understand. It gave her an excuse to enlarge on a favourite theme of hers, the need for understanding within a community such as Addendon; the need to 'build bridges'.

'We all know,' she said, 'how easy it is for misunderstandings and petty squabbles to arise in a town such as Addendon, where the population has increased so rapidly within the last few years. It's so easy for the original inhabitants to resent the new-comers and for the newcomers not to see the point of view of the original inhabitants. I see my job, as one of the leaders of the community, as helping to build bridges.'

Her audience, who'd heard all this before, was getting restive. But not Annabel. Kate noticed that she was now staring raptly at Mrs Stringer.

'Yes, building bridges. Mr – er – the Director of – er – has spoken of international peace and understanding. Perhaps some of us feel a little helpless about that, wondering what we can do. Well, I'll tell you. We can concentrate on soothing the little everyday quarrels around us. Do that and the world will become a happier place. Solve the little problems and the big ones will melt away. This can be our contribution to international understanding.'

'Old fraud,' muttered Kate. 'Dad says she's stirred up more –'

'Sssh!' hissed Annabel fiercely. Kate looked at her in surprise.

'It may not be easy,' Mrs Stringer ended shrilly. 'Worthwhile things never are. We may have to suffer for our beliefs – I know I always have. But I shall continue to try to build bridges and I hope I can inspire you to do the same.'

She sat down, red-faced, almost on the lap of the Deputy Director of whatever-it-was, whose existence she had forgotten. He managed to move aside just in time.

There was a general surge towards the food. Then above the noise sounded a lonely burst of hand-clapping. It came from Annabel, who had remained motionless.

'Oh, come on, Annabel,' said Kate, glancing round

shame-faced, hoping that no one was looking, 'all the best cakes'll be gone.'

'She's right, Kate,' said Annabel, unexpectedly. 'They're both right. I'm going to congratulate them.'

To Kate's astonishment, she went over and engaged Mrs Stringer and the Deputy Director in earnest conversation.

Kate got on with the urgent business of cornering enough refreshments for both of them.

'What were you saying to them?' she asked, when Annabel rejoined her.

'I just told them how inspiring I thought they were,' replied Annabel. 'I said to Mrs Stringer that from now on I'm right behind her.'

She shovelled some canapés into her mouth thoughtfully.

'You know, Kate, this may be the cause I've been looking for. It's a funny thing but just over the last few days I've been thinking about what life's for. Is it really just about going to school and sitting around watching television? Is there nothing more to it than that?

'And then, suddenly, Mrs Stringer points the way. Where's the coffee? Don't say it's all gone!'

Annabel was unusually silent after that. As they left the hall shortly afterwards she was lost in thought.

She remained so all the way back until, nearing Oakwood Crescent again, the sound of yells and grunts was borne faintly on the breeze.

'It's those boys, Kate,' she said. 'They're still fighting.'

'Don't I know,' groaned Kate. 'They never stop. They'll be there till it gets dark.'

A light had appeared in Annabel's eye and she

hurried forward more quickly until the boys came into view.

They seemed tireless. The Green resembled a snake-pit as they writhed and wrestled in a constantly shifting heap. Annabel paused and eyed it with an expression compounded of distaste and satisfaction.

'You remember what Mrs Stringer said, Kate? *Concentrate on soothing the little everyday quarrels around us. Solve the little problems and the big ones will melt away.*'

'Well, yes, but –'

'I've been wondering where I might find a problem to help solve and maybe this is it. I expect it's only an everyday little quarrel but it's my chance to do something about peace and understanding. Since nobody else has bothered to find out what they're fighting about, I'm going to.'

Well! Kate didn't remind her of what she'd said earlier in the evening – there wasn't time.

'Stop fighting!' yelled Annabel, advancing upon the heaving mass, 'and tell me what the quarrel's about. Whatever it is I'm sure it can be settled in a friendly fashion.'

Her voice was drowned in the uproar. Annabel went close and tugged at some shoulders. Her voice rose higher still.

'I SAID "STOP –"'

Like a rugger scrum, the heap fell back on her and she was swallowed up.

Kate started forward in alarm but she needn't have worried. The boys realized almost immediately that there was a foreign body in their midst and she was ejected again.

Although Annabel only had herself to blame the boys were all very apologetic. As she rose stiffly to her feet, she was surrounded by anxious faces.

'You all right?' enquired a thin, pale-faced boy wearing brown corduroy trousers and a rollneck sweater.

'Sorry,' said a stout, perspiring boy with big ears dressed in blue jeans and a tee shirt.

'It's quite all right, thanks,' said Annabel, a little huffily but mollified by their politeness.

'In that case –' said Paleface, turning to glare at Big Ears –

'We'll get back to –' began Big Ears, returning the glare with interest.

'Wait!' Annabel cut in hastily. She stepped between them. 'Just tell me what you're fighting about. I'm here to help in the cause of international understanding.'

Both Paleface and Big Ears looked flattered.

'Well, if you're really interested,' said Big Ears, 'it's like this. We're the Oakwood Crescent gang and this is our Green. This is where we play. And they're trying to take it from us.'

His voice became heated as he spoke and he pointed an accusing finger at Paleface.

'What do you say to that?' Annabel asked Paleface. He looked Big Ears contemptuously up and down.

'We,' he said, coldly, 'are the Mill Lane Gang. But the people on Mill Lane won't let us play on our Green so we have to come to this rotten place –'

'If it's so rotten why come?' demanded Big Ears shrilly. There were mutterings of agreement among his followers and a general shuffling as both gangs braced themselves for further action.

'Now wait, wait, wait,' cried Annabel importantly. 'How will we ever get international understanding if you're so touchy?' She turned to Kate.

77

'You see, Kate, it's as I thought. This isn't just a pointless quarrel. There's a genuine problem here which would never have come to light if I hadn't made it my business to find out.'

She turned back to the boys.

'Now the situation is that if the Mill Lane gang were allowed to play on their own Green, as the Oakwood Crescent gang have always been allowed to play on theirs, there wouldn't be any need to quarrel. Isn't that so, boys?'

'That's right, miss,' glowed Paleface.

'Good riddance!' sneered Big Ears.

'So like most of the problems in this modern world, it could easily be solved if only somebody would apply a little common sense. And I mean to see that it is solved. The Mill Lane gang *shall* be allowed to play on their own Green. I shall attend to it personally.'

'Thanks, miss,' gasped Paleface, admiringly.

'Now it's getting dark so you may as well go home. Just leave this to me.'

They all ran off with whoops and yells and sublime peace settled for the evening on Oakwood Crescent.

It was all very well for Annabel to be so grand but she knew Mill Lane perfectly well and if she'd given the matter just a few seconds' proper thought she'd have realized that it wasn't as simple as all that.

The top end of Mill Lane – that is, the old part round the Green – is the snobbiest part of Addendon. It wasn't going to be easy to persuade the people there to throw the Green open to a lot of yelling hooligans from the bottom end where the new houses are.

Annabel and Kate went to inspect the Mill Lane Green on the following evening. Unlike the Oakwood Crescent Green, which is just a triangular patch of scrubby grass, the Mill Lane Green had class:

rustic seats, chestnut trees and flowering cherries and the old Mill Pond cleaned up and with water lilies on it: plus some *Keep Off The Grass* signs.

Having absorbed all that, Annabel turned her attention to the houses that were dotted on either side of the Green. They were biggish, set in their own grounds, and had refinements like mock Tudor gables, leaded windows and brass knockers. A far cry from the semis of Oakwood Crescent, and one could sense the power that lay behind those posh front doors – the power that managed to keep their Green free from uncouth gangs of shouting boys while lesser streets like Oakwood Crescent had to submit.

Even Annabel looked thoughtful.

'It's not going to be easy, Kate,' she conceded. 'But in the great cause of international understanding I shall do it.'

By the following day it looked even less easy.

'We have to concentrate on soothing the little everyday quarrels around us,' Annabel was saying hoarsely. 'Solve the little problems and the big ones will melt away. This can be *your* contribution to international understanding.'

Annabel was on a Mill Lane doorstep. Kate hovered, nervous and cowardly, behind her.

'As far as I can see,' said the owner of the doorstep, 'you are adding to the world's quarrels instead of soothing them. Or you are about to, unless you go quickly.'

He was elderly, stooping and well-bred. In one hand he held a Sunday newspaper and he had obviously been enjoying a Sunday afternoon nap until Annabel had come to bother him like some persistent blue-bottle.

'You mean you won't –'

'No.'

The door slammed.

'Miserable lot,' snarled Annabel.

'No one's agreed yet and there's only one house left,' said Kate. 'It hardly seems worth bothering about that one.'

'We are *not* giving up,' snapped Annabel.

The last house was the most splendid of the lot: real Georgian, dripping with old coach lamps and wrought iron gates and surrounded by lawns and shrubberies. Annabel leaned on the bell and went into her speech while the door was still half open.

'The great need in Addendon,' she began, 'is to build bridges –'

Then she looked into the face of the woman who had opened the door and her mouth fell open.

It was Mrs Stringer.

'I – I didn't know you lived in Mill Lane,' she stammered.

'Lived here for thirty years,' said Mrs Stringer, beaming importantly. 'Heavens, girls, I'm Chairman of the Residents' Association.'

'Chairman of the – the – of the –' whispered Annabel, sounding like a sticking gramophone record, 'yes, I – I suppose you would be. Mrs Stringer, I wonder if I could come inside. There's such a lot to talk about and my feet are killing me.'

'So you see,' said Annabel, some ten minutes later, 'it was your magnificent speech at the meeting that inspired me to do this. I told you I was going to get right behind you and I am . . . and so is my friend Kate. You were right about having to suffer for one's beliefs as well but we don't mind, do we, Kate, not as long as you are here to inspire and lead.'

Mrs Stringer cleared her throat. She didn't look

very inspiring just then. The important look had gone.

They were in Mrs Stringer's sitting room. A small, elderly man sitting in an armchair by the fireplace had looked over his newspaper and smiled and nodded shyly at them when they had entered, then gone back behind it again. He was, presumably, Mr Stringer, though Mrs Stringer had not introduced him or otherwise shown any awareness of his existence.

'As I understand it,' twittered Mrs Stringer, doubtfully, 'you want me to use my position as Chairman of the Residents' Association to ensure that the – the ban on children playing on the Green will be lifted and the – the Mill Lane gang in particular be allowed on there. In the cause of – of building bridges and international understanding.'

'That's it!' cried Annabel enthusiastically.

'You know I don't really think that would be possible. They are high class people round here and I'm afraid most of them don't have my social conscience; *uncaring* people, many of them, I'm sorry to say. And they don't like children making a lot of noise . . . they'd need a lot of persuading.'

'I *know*,' cried Annabel passionately. 'But *you* could do it, a person of *your* influence and leadership and gift of the gab. And after that speech at the meeting you've got to try, haven't you? I mean, it wouldn't do if it got round Addendon that you don't practise what you preach. Not that it would, of course, but you know what I mean.'

Mrs Stringer gave Annabel a narrow look, then heaved her bulk out of her chair and paced ponderously up and down. She appeared agitated. When she spoke it was in a lowered voice.

'There's nothing that I, personally, should like better but –' she nodded confidentially towards the figure in the armchair – 'it's my husband – not well – needs quiet –' She nodded and winked and held up a forefinger to indicate that she didn't want to say too much in case he should overhear. While she was doing this, the newspaper was lowered.

'That's quite all right, Winnie dear. I wouldn't mind. I'd like it. It'd be nice to see something out of the window in the evenings. It gets lonely at times with you out at so many meetings.'

He disappeared behind his newspaper again. He appeared to Kate to be smiling triumphantly but perhaps she was mistaken.

Mrs Stringer stiffened and shuddered as if stabbed in the back. Then she moved to the window and looked out at the Green. It looked beautiful with the sunshine glinting on it. Beautiful and peaceful. She sighed deeply.

'Yes,' she said to Annabel. 'Yes, I know what you mean.'

The newspaper gave a little rustle.

Four days later, an extraordinary meeting of the Upper Mill Lane Residents' Association decided grudgingly, by one vote, that the Mill Lane children would be allowed to play on their Green. Mrs Stringer had done her stuff.

Annabel was overjoyed, of course, and determined to make the most of her triumph. Nothing less than a grand opening ceremony would do and Mrs Stringer, who felt that if she were going to make some sacrifices she ought at least to receive her reward in publicity, was easily persuaded. The *Addendon Weekly Advertiser* was invited.

Paleface and the Mill Lane gang were equally overjoyed and suggested that for her services Annabel should be appointed President of the gang. Annabel declined, however, saying that it would be wrong for her to seem to be attached to any particular group.

Still, it was all very heady and Kate could see that Annabel's mind was moving on to bigger things.

'As I said, Kate, it only needs a little applied common sense and effort,' she told Kate for the umpteenth time as they made their way to Mill Lane Green for the opening ceremony. 'When I look at the state the world's in today just because of a lack of common sense I want to weep. I mean to go on from here.'

It was a lovely evening for the ceremony. The Mill Lane gang were all there with Paleface standing in front of them. Some of the Mill Lane residents had come to watch apprehensively and there were a few other spectators, presumably passers-by who had nothing better to do. Still, an audience to Mrs Stringer was anything that had ears and she could never resist an opportunity for a speech.

With Annabel standing modestly on one side and Kate on the other, she spoke of the new, caring spirit which was emerging in Mill Lane. She hoped that she wouldn't be thought boastful if she claimed to be at any rate partly responsible for this. It augured well, she thought, for the prospect of building bridges between the old community and the new.

She also complimented Annabel, saying that if she – Mrs Stringer – never did anything else in public life, she would rest content knowing that she had been able to inspire at least one young person to follow the same ideals as herself. She then declared the Green open to the Mill Lane children.

'They will be free,' she announced, 'to play here whenever they want.'

'Hip, hip!' screeched Paleface, following Annabel's instructions.

'Hooray!' yelled the gang, in ragged chorus.

'Hip, hip!'

Before the second cheer could get going, there was a commotion somewhere behind Kate and she spun round to see the Oakwood Crescent gang racing into view.

'C-H-A-R-G-E!' screamed Big Ears, who was in the lead.

'Repel attack!' rapped Paleface, his experienced eye sizing up the situation at a glance.

Suddenly, there they were again, the two gangs locked in battle but this time on the Mill Lane Green.

Annabel took it as a personal affront. Before Mrs Stringer or any of the other spectators had gathered their wits she was advancing indignantly upon the fray. Big Ears was struggling joyously on the edge of it and Annabel, pushing aside a Mill Lane gangster, grabbed him by the back of his sweater.

'Why do you have to fight now?' she screamed. 'You've each got a green, haven't you? Isn't that what you've always wanted?'

The squirming heap fell backwards on Annabel again and she disappeared from view. She came crawling out, red-faced, a moment later and Kate gave her a helping hand.

Big Ears' grinning, perspiring face appeared out of the heap for just one moment.

'Because they've got a better Green than we have now. We want to play on their Green.'

He disappeared from view again.

'Surely you remember, Annabel,' said Kate, as she yanked her away, 'all healthy boys of that age must fight. They enjoy it. It's part of their nature.'

And that's how Oakwood Crescent got rid of the boys fighting in their Green. The Crescent was deliciously peaceful again after that. Annabel instantly became very popular in Oakwood Crescent and everyone smiled at her and said Hallo when she went to call for Kate.

It was a pity that she didn't feel able to go up Mill Lane for a while. But then it doesn't really lead anywhere much.

The boys continued to fight every evening on the Mill Lane Green. The racket was quite unbelievable.

The Bunce saga

*****

'Annabel,' said Kate.

'Yes?' said Annabel.

'When are you going to tell me why your middle name's Fidelity? You're always saying you're going to but you never do.'

Annabel didn't reply. Kate's had been an idle, non-urgent sort of question which didn't really call for any response. Like Kate, Annabel was gazing dreamily into space, though *thoughtfully* might have been a better word in her case.

It was the aftermath of Angela Dill's party and Annabel and Kate were seated at the table in the Dills' big farmhouse kitchen, which was still strewn with present wrappings and burst balloons, waiting for Kate's father to come and drive them home. The Dills lived in the country about three miles from Addendon. Angela and her mother were presumably outside, waving off departing guests.

The only other remaining guest, Miles Noggins, sat sprawled in a chair opposite Annabel and Kate, his face flushed and bloated, his eyes glazed. Occasionally, slight gasps emanated from him but otherwise he hardly stirred and when he did make a slight movement it clearly hurt. He was over-fed. He, too, was waiting for a parent to take him home but how they were going to get him in the car when they arrived was not easy to see. Perhaps he would have to be carried. But presumably it was not a new problem for Mr and Mrs Noggins.

'I just thought,' said Kate, after a further period of silence, 'that while we're sitting here waiting for Dad to arrive, it would pass the time if you told me. But I can see you're thinking about something else.'

'I am,' said Annabel.

She was thinking about food and that Mrs Dill must rank amongst the best cooks she had ever encountered. The party food that afternoon, both savoury and sweet, had been so utterly fantastic, so incredibly out of this world, that it was worth going back mentally over it all and reviving memories.

However, she was also feeling a little disgruntled. She could have done with more. She had a feeling that when everybody else had been grabbing, she had been too lady-like and missed out. She was regretting it now, especially when she looked at Miles Noggins and reflected upon how successfully he must have grabbed.

She didn't pity his present condition. She envied it.

In particular, her mind kept on going back to the raspberry trifle. It had been the most superb thing she had ever tasted. She had had one but she knew that some people had had two. She suspected that Miles Noggins had had three, perhaps four.

She closed her eyes in order to visualize a raspberry trifle more clearly. Yes, she could see it vividly. Seen through its glass dish it had different coloured layers, all of an extraordinary succulence, covered by a snowfall of cream with nuts and strips of other delicious things strewn on top –

Hearing footsteps, Annabel opened her eyes and

found that the vision had become, as if by a miracle, flesh. She was looking straight at a real raspberry trifle. Mrs Dill was standing in the kitchen doorway, holding it.

'Are you three the only ones left?' beamed Mrs Dill. 'Look, I've just found this. Perhaps one of you would like to finish it up if you're not too full already. Fight it out between you which one has it.'

She put the trifle down on the table and left the kitchen.

There was silence for a moment as Annabel's mind adjusted to the situation.

'What about you, Kate?' she inquired.

'I just couldn't,' Kate said wistfully. 'Couldn't. I'm so full . . .'

'Oh, well,' said Annabel brightly. She looked at Miles Noggins. 'I expect you're too full as well, aren't you?'

The bloated face twitched indignantly and found a voice.

'Course I'm not. What do you mean? Too full!'

'You mean you want it?'

'Course I want it.'

Annabel closed her eyes for a moment.

'Perhaps we could share it then,' she said when she opened them again.

'Half of it wouldn't be worth having.'

Annabel closed her eyes again.

'Then how do you think we should – er –'

'I dunno. What about tossing for it?'

Annabel gazed at the raspberry trifle. Then she sighed, got up and walked over to the sink. She leant her elbows on the draining board and, back towards the others, gazed out of the window.

'You asked me, Kate,' she said, after a while, 'to tell you why my middle name is Fidelity. I've decided that I'm going to do so. I've kept it secret for a long time but now I feel the time is ripe.'

'What about the trifle?' said Miles, indignant at the change of subject.

'You can't be in that much of a hurry,' said Annabel. 'You're lucky you haven't burst already. We shall decide about the trifle when I have told you my story.'

'Well, hurry up, then,' he said, churlishly.

Annabel ignored him. Instead, she continued to gaze out of the window. It was as if she were plucking up courage. When at last she spoke again it was in a lowered voice.

'I warn you, it's a very tragic story. We Bunces haven't always lived in Badger's Close, you know.'

'I didn't think you had,' said Kate, puzzled. 'The houses were only built about seven years ago.'

'I mean, in places *like* Badger's Close. We've come down in the world. We're a fallen family.'

Pausing to let her words sink in, Annabel noticed that some peanuts had been spilt on the draining board. They looked as though they might have got a little bit damp and, thoughtfully, she tested one for softness with her finger.

'Like I said, I've never told anybody this and it may be that Mum and Dad won't be very pleased about it when they find out. But I just can't not talk about it any longer. In the middle part of the last century the Bunces were wealthy, one of the richest and most powerful families in the land. They had connections at court and some people said they were the real power behind our foreign policy –'

'Is this a long story?' grunted Miles, morosely.

'And yet,' continued Annabel, ignoring him, 'by the end of the century, all this fantastic power and wealth had melted away. Why? What had happened?

Well might you ask, Kate, and you, Miles. So you see when you ask me why I'm called Fidelity, it's not as simple as you think. What you're really asking me to do is tell you the story of what you might call the decline and fall of the House of Bunce.'

The peanut seemed to be all right. She chewed it thoughtfully.

'I don't know why you have to tell it now, but at least get on with it,' said Miles. 'If you don't hurry up, somebody else might come in and want this trifle.'

'I shall tell it as quickly and simply as I can,' said Annabel.

'How come the Bunces were so rich?' asked Kate. 'What had they made their money out of?'

'Cotton,' said Annabel. 'Originally the Bunces were a Yorkshire family.'

'But I thought it was wool in Yorkshire, cotton in Lancashire.'

'You're right, Kate, so right, you always are. But there are just a few parts of Yorkshire where it was cotton. Important parts, though. Just over the border from Lancashire.'

She selected another peanut.

'It was old Ebenezer Bunce who founded the family fortune. And as the family got bigger and spread out everywhere he used to control everything, like a spider at the centre of its web, sitting there in his big smoke-blackened house on top of a ridge of the Pennines on the Yorkshire-Lancashire border.

'He was a man of fantastic energy, spending his weekdays going round the mills encouraging the workers – because he was a very enlightened employer was Ebenezer Bunce – then in the evenings and at weekends he'd go back to Hardstone Hall and stride up and down the bogs and moors making his

90

decisions. There's a story that once he stood on the top of Blackbog Fell and shook his fist into the screaming wind and sleet and shouted a mighty oath. He shouted – "Ah, Ebenezer Boonce, swear that ah wunna rest till t'Boonces are t'greatest family in t'land after t'Queen." My accent isn't very good but it was something like that. He screamed it right into this tearing wind.'

'Why was Hardstone Hall smoke-blackened when it was on top of a ridge in the Pennines?' asked Miles, in a surly tone of voice. He was beginning to take a grudging interest in spite of himself.

'Because,' said Annabel, 'it was built from the stones of one of his mills which had been demolished to make way for a better one. I told you he was a very enlightened employer for those days but then he didn't want to waste the stone. But, anyway, that's another story in itself and I don't intend to go into that now.'

She gave Miles a severe look as though to admonish him for interrupting, then selected another peanut.

'So how did the decline start?' asked Kate.

'I was just getting to that. In a way, though perhaps you won't believe this, it started when old Ebenezer and Emily moved to London – Emily was his wife. Course, at the time it didn't seem like that at all. It seemed like a triumphal procession. Old Ebenezer knew that he'd gone as far as he could in Yorkshire. If he were to make good his oath he had to move near to the centre of power. He had to be close to the Queen and to Parliament. It was expected that very soon he'd be made a peer and he'd have to take his seat in the House of Lords . . .

'So they moved to this grand house in Belgrave Square with flocks of servants and nannies taking all the little Bunces for walks in Hyde Park.'

'Were there a lot of little Bunces?' asked Kate. 'I mean, who did they belong to?'

'Quite a lot. They were Ebenezer's children and grandchildren. You know what big families the Victorians had.'

'All living in the one house in Belgrave Square?'

'Oh, no. Gradually, you see, the Bunces were buying all the houses in Belgrave Square. Ebenezer's children were growing up and having children of their own and getting big, important jobs. They all had posh accents but they still all recognized him as the leader of the Bunces, sitting there in his wheelchair with his long white beard.

'The Bunces had the world at their feet. They were almost running the country, but Ebenezer was worried. He felt that the fire was going out of them and they were getting soft with all that luxury. And he still had to make good his oath. You see, the Bunces were very *nearly* the most powerful family in the land after the Queen but there was one other family that still stood in the way. This other family wasn't like the Bunces – it had been around for a long time and they were a lot of smoothies. They didn't like to see the upstart Bunces catching them up and there was a sort of unspoken rivalry between the two families.'

'That must have been a very interesting situation,' said Kate.

'It was,' replied Annabel.

'What was the name of this other family?'

Annabel picked up another peanut from the draining board, put it in her mouth, then turned and, arms folded and head bowed, began to walk very slowly up and down the kitchen. She appeared to be undergoing some emotional stress.

'I'm afraid I'm not going to tell you that yet,' she

said at length. 'I'm going to keep it a secret until the end of my story. Then I shall reveal it. Till then I'm going to refer to the other family as "Family X".'

'Gosh!' said Kate. 'Why? Is there a reason?'

'You shall see the reason in good time,' replied Annabel mysteriously.

'Did your ancestors really own a lot of houses in Belgrave Square?' asked Miles in an awed voice. He was cottoning on slowly.

'Practically the whole square, and Knightsbridge, too,' Annabel replied abstractedly. 'But to get back to the point. As I was saying, old Ebenezer was getting worried. He'd got this sense of doom, this foreboding that something terrible was going to happen. He'd always been so powerful, a man of steel, but now he began to wake up groaning and sweating in the middle of the night and he'd say "Em'ly lass, where art tha? Where art tha?" and she'd say "Doan't thee worry, Ebenezer lad, I'm right 'ere. What's troubling thee, thee that was so strong and mighty?" and all that.

'And he'd toss about and say "I've been 'aving this dream, Em'ly lass, this terrible dream. It's a warning. We ought to get back to where we belong, back t' t' Yorkshire-Lancashire border. There's nowt for us 'ere in t' soft south, nowt."'

'What?'

'"There's nowt for us 'ere in t' soft south, nowt."'

'How do you know just what they said?' asked Miles, suspiciously.

'Because Emily told her children, of course. And they passed it on from generation to generation. It's part of the Bunce legend.'

'So what did Emily say to that?' asked Kate, eagerly.

'She'd say "Nay, lad, nay. Tha knows tha munna go

back. Tha knows tha must fulfil tha destiny or dee."
She was thinking only of him, you see. Then she'd
straighten his nightcap and sing him back to sleep
with a lullaby.'

'But he was right, wasn't he?' said Kate.

Annabel stopped her pacing and went back to the
draining board. Placing her elbows on it, she bent her
face down low over it and held it there in silence. Kate
wondered for a moment if she had broken down and
was in tears and she started up in some alarm. Then
Annabel straightened up, holding a peanut, which
she popped into her mouth. She had been groping for
it in the crack behind the draining board.

'Yes, he was right,' she said, then she fell silent
again.

Her back was towards Kate and Miles but watching
her, Kate saw that Annabel's chin was lifting, her
shoulders squaring. When she spoke again, there was
a certain pride in her voice.

'And the cause of the downfall was Fidelity. My
namesake, Fidelity.'

'We're getting to the point then at last, are we?' said
Miles, whose thoughts had begun to revert to the
raspberry trifle.

'And – and who was Fidelity?' asked Kate.

'She was Ebenezer's grand-daughter. She'd always
been his favourite grandchild right from when he'd
dandled her on his rough old knee. And by the time
she was seventeen she was his pride and joy. "The
flower of the Bunces" he used to call her. Because she
was really lovely and talented and kind and – and just
everything, really. The whole world adored her.'

A melancholy expression settled on Annabel's face
as she thought of her namesake.

It had dimly dawned upon Miles that Annabel had
found a source of peanuts on the draining board and a

surge of greed passed through him. Placing one hand on the table, he struggled heavily to get to his feet but couldn't make it and subsided again, sullenly.

Annabel gave up the peanuts and sat down between Miles and Kate. The melancholy, abstracted expression was still on her face.

'It gets hard to tell this part,' she said. 'I have to sit down and – and sort of steel myself. Just be patient for a sec.

'There!' she said, after a few moments, 'I'm all right now but I warn you – it's a bit harrowing. As you know, even you, Miles, the name Fidelity means Faith. And Fidelity lived up to her name all right. She certainly did.

'Anyway, when Fidelity was seventeen she made this announcement to the rest of the Bunce family. She'd decided that she wanted to go on the stage and secretly she'd been looking for a job in the chorus. It seemed she'd been giving her governess the slip and putting on common clothes and imitating a cockney accent and –'

'Why'd she do all that?' inquired Miles, who was becoming interested again.

'Because in those days young ladies of quality didn't go on the stage, of course. They used to sit at home doing their tapestries and looking modest. So when, at that meeting in their house in Grosvenor Gardens –'

'I thought the Bunces lived in Belgrave Square and Knightsbridge.'

'For goodness' sake, they were spreading all the time. They were into Park Lane by now. So when she told everybody what she'd done, of course, there was consternation. If it hadn't been for Ebenezer, her parents would probably have thrown her out into the street in disgrace, or at least found some way of stopping it, but old Ebenezer had always loved her and there was this great scene when – when –' Annabel was stumbling over words and there was a catch in her voice but she managed to recover her poise – 'when in the great dining room of Fidelity's home, among all the assembled Bunces all shouting against Fidelity and telling her she was disgracing the family, old Ebenezer got to his feet and raised his hand high –'

'You said Ebenezer was in a wheelchair,' protested Miles.

'Got to his feet with difficulty and in great pain and cried: "Let the lass be! There's a new age a-coming and we Bunces have got to be part of it."'

'Women's Lib,' said Kate, impressed.

'That's right. Old Ebenezer was one of the first to see it coming. And all the Bunces fell silent at the sound of that mighty voice. He was still the leader of them and they couldn't stand against him ... but when he fell back into his wheelchair he was – he was crying like a baby because – because he knew ...'

Annabel seemed to be on the verge of crying herself. She rested her elbows on the table and put her hands to her forehead.

'Because he knew somewhere deep inside him that this was all part of the coming tragedy. The Bunces,' said Annabel, lifting her eyes nobly to the ceiling, 'were marching inexorably towards their doom, like – like characters in a Greek tragedy.'

Miles was quite affected by this. He gaped at her, mouth wide open, trifle and peanuts temporarily forgotten.

'So Fidelity went on the stage. And within months she was the toast of London. There were queues outside all the theatres where she played – the Gaiety, the Alhambra, the – the – oh, I can't remember them all. But her name was on everybody's lips.'

'But she was only a chorus girl, wasn't she?' said Kate.

'Yes, but that just shows you – what a chorus girl! Every night she was snowed under by the flowers. The world was at her feet. She seemed to have a fantastic future before her and even the Bunces who'd been so opposed to her going on the stage were silenced and then –'

'And then what?' said Miles after a time. Annabel had covered her face with her hands and lapsed into silence.

'Then this – this *rotter* came into her life.'

'*Rotter?*'

'Yes.'

'Who was he?'

Annabel was now clearly undergoing great emotion. Her face was completely hidden behind her hands. Miles sat staring at her, mouth still hanging open, an unlovely sight.

'His Christian name was Albert. His surname I can't tell you yet because – and this was the extraordinary thing – he was from the family I told you about – the one family in the land that was still more important than the Bunces – the one family that still stood in the way of Ebenezer's great vow.'

'You mean,' said Kate, 'the family you called X?'

'That's right. So for the time being let's call him Albert X. He was a really smooth charmer was Albert X, but he wasn't only that. He was a bit older than Fidelity but still not very old and already he was in Parliament, in fact he was in the Government and in fact' – Annabel lowered her voice – 'he was favourite to be the next Prime Minister, when the present one – his name was Disraeli – decided to call it a day.'

'Haw!' said Miles, deeply impressed, his mouth sagging still further and his eyes rounding.

'So there was this Albert X, twirling his moustache and rolling his eyes and sending her flowers and escorting her to Gilbert and Sullivan musicals – and she fell madly in love with him. She worshipped the ground he walked on. When he proposed to her, she accepted like a shot.'

'But getting married to him would have united the two families,' said Kate. 'Together, the Bunces and the Xs would have made far and away the most powerful family in the country.'

'You're right, Kate, so right as usual, and that's what the Bunces thought. After all their opposition to Fidelity's going on the stage, now they decided it had been a good thing after all and everybody started getting excited and preparing for the wedding.

'It was going to be the wedding of the year, the union between the Bunces and the Xs. Queen Victoria herself was going to be there, so was the Prime Minister and all the Cabinet, Charles Dickens, Gilbert and Sullivan, Charlie Chaplin.'

'Charlie Chaplin!' said Kate. 'What year was this?'

But Annabel hadn't heard. Increasingly, as she'd been speaking, there had been a catch in her voice and now she seemed too overcome by emotion to go on. From behind her hands were coming muffled sobs.

'The wedding was only two weeks away when – when –'

'Yeah?' said Miles, leaning forward, carried away now by the story.

'– when the anonymous letter arrived.'

'Anonymous letter!' said Kate. 'What about? Arrived where?'

'It was sent to Fidelity and signed – signed "A

well-wisher". It said that Albert was a ne'er-do-well, a rotter who was deceiving her. It said – it said –'

'Yes?'

'That he already had a wife.'

'What did Fidelity do?'

'She swooned and had the vapours. They had to call the doctor and nobody knew what was wrong with her because she didn't tell anybody – not *anybody* – not at first, anyway. Not until she told Albert himself.'

'Albert! But did she believe this letter or what?'

'No. She didn't believe it. She had absolute trust in Albert. And of course he put his hand on his heart and told her it was all lies. But he didn't have to convince her. She only even bothered to show him the letter because she thought he had an enemy and he ought to know that. She was worried that this enemy would carry on spreading lies about Albert.'

'She'd no idea who wrote this letter, I suppose,' said Kate.

'Well, she didn't know who'd sent it but she knew where it came from because the person who'd written it had absent-mindedly used a bit of paper with an address on the back of it – an address in Lambeth –'

'That was *very* absent-minded, wasn't it?'

'Yes. But then you must remember that this letter was written under great stress.'

Annabel looked under great stress herself. She rose suddenly and started pacing up and down again. She was twisting her hands nervously against each other.

'Anyway, Albert persuaded Fidelity not to do anything about this letter. He just laughed at it and said that some harmless crank must have written it. So Fidelity managed to push it out of her mind until – until –'

'Yes?'

Annabel's voice was becoming steadily more anguished.

'It was the day of the wedding. Fidelity got ready early, all dressed up in her beautiful wedding gown. She knew that at Westminster Abbey –'

'Westminster Abbey!' echoed Miles. 'Gaw!'

'At Westminster Abbey all the Bunces and Xs would be gathering early, too, ready for the historic joining of the two families. And suddenly – and suddenly she couldn't stand it. She had to know that her darling Albert was safe from this person who was spreading such malicious rumours about him – rumours which if anybody believed them might stop him from becoming the next Prime Minister. So do you know what she did? She ran out into the street and called a hansom cab.'

'In her wedding dress?'

'Yes. And in this cab she travelled to that address in Lambeth, to a mean little house in a mean street, and there she found, crouched in a corner half-starved, dressed in rags – she found –'

'Yes, go on,' cried Kate and Miles in unison as Annabel appeared to be about to break down altogether.

'– the person who'd written that letter – this poor creature – that rotter Albert X's *wife*.'

Annabel closed her eyes and there was silence.

'Then – then it was his wife,' said Kate, breathlessly. 'There wasn't any doubt about it.'

'None. This person was able to show the marriage certificate. She was able to tell Fidelity how he'd abused her and flung her ruthlessly out into the street and how she didn't want the same thing to happen to Fidelity. But that was only the beginning. Because as Fidelity stood there struck dumb with horror, in burst Albert and – and –'

'What?' cried Miles. Annabel seemed unable to go on. She was convulsed by great sobs. Then she steadied herself.

'He was in a terrible rage. He was holding a shotgun. And as Fidelity watched, screaming with horror, he raised it to his shoulder and killed the poor woman. Killed her.'

'Baw-w-w!' said Miles, eyes bulging.

'But wait till you hear what happened next. It was then that Fidelity lived up to her name – and mine. Do you know what she did –'

'Course we don't,' said Miles. 'Come on, tell, tell.'

'She snatched the smoking shotgun from Albert X and ran out in the street in her wedding dress. He was in a panic now that he'd done it, the coward, and he ran after her begging and pleading with her not to tell anybody. But she didn't even seem to hear him. She kept on running, right through all the mean streets and over Westminster Bridge. And her wedding dress was getting all filthy and sweaty or it would have got sweaty if Fidelity hadn't been too lovely to sweat. And then – and then –'

Miles' eyes were bulging still further out. His mouth hung open and slobbering rattles and gurgles, the outward signs of the emotions raging within him, issued from it.

'Yes?' whispered Kate.

'As Big Ben struck the hour when the wedding was to take place, Fidelity staggered into Westminster Abbey with Albert pursuing her. Everybody rose to their feet, shrieking –'

'Even Queen Victoria – and Gilbert and Sullivan?' breathed Miles.

'Everybody. And then – and then –'

Annabel suddenly covered her face with her hands again and burst into sobs. Kate jumped to her feet.

'There, there,' she said soothingly, patting Annabel on the shoulder.

'Sorry,' whispered Annabel, lowering her hands. 'It – it gets a bit hard to tell. But I'll try – I'll try –'

'Come on,' said Miles, impatiently. 'What happened?'

'In front of everybody, Fidelity flung the shotgun to the ground and cried out "I have killed a woman."'

There was a silence.

'You mean –' said Kate, at last.

'She took the blame on herself. She knew now that Albert was a rotter but she was so much in love with him that she couldn't help herself. She still wanted Albert to go on and become Prime Minister . . .

'And Albert was such a rotten coward that he let her do it.'

'So – so what happened in the end?'

'Of course, the rest of the Bunces stood by her, especially old Ebenezer. They didn't believe she'd done it and they tried to get her to change her story but she wouldn't . . . They hired the best lawyers in London and paid out millions of pounds . . .

'The Bunces ruined themselves raising the money to defend Fidelity. They had to sell up their houses in Belgrave Square and Park Lane and so on and move to digs in Clapham and places like that. The family was brought to its knees.

'But it didn't save Fidelity. She – she was found guilty and hanged. And her last words were, "I shall always love Albert. He will be a great Prime Minister."'

Another profound silence descended. It was broken by Miles.

'The rotter,' he said.

'Ebenezer died, too,' said Annabel. 'He was a broken man whose only thought was vengeance. On the day that Fidelity died, he pursued Albert down Ludgate Hill and his wheelchair went out of control and he crashed . . .

'But it wasn't the crash that did it. The doctors said afterwards it was a broken heart.'

'What a terrible, terrible story,' said Kate.

'There were bodies everywhere. Like *Macbeth*. And all because of that rotter Albert X.'

'What happened to him?' asked Miles. 'Did he become Prime Minister? His real name wasn't Gladstone, was it?'

'No. He never became Prime Minister. That, perhaps, is the strangest thing of all about this whole strange story.'

Kate observed that, in the midst of her violent grief, Annabel, who had wandered over to the draining board again, had found another peanut and was chewing it.

'Everything suddenly started going wrong for this X family as well. It wasn't one thing. It was lots of things. They all started losing their money and they had to sell out and move to Clapham and Balham as well. And Albert was never made Prime Minister. He lost his seat in Parliament at the next election and died in lonely and penniless obscurity.'

'Serves him right,' said Miles. 'But it was funny, wasn't it?'

'That's what everybody thought,' said Annabel. 'There was a lot of whispering about it. Fingers were pointed at the Xs. It began to be said that they had done a terrible wrong to the Bunces and that now there was a curse on them. A legend grew —'

'Quite right, too,' said Miles.

'I'm glad you think so,' said Annabel.

'Well, course I do. Wouldn't anybody?' said Miles. Then as something about Annabel's tone of voice penetrated into his food-fuddled brain he said – 'What do you mean? – glad I think so?'

Annabel ignored him.

'A legend grew that the Xs would remain cursed until the day that one of their number made recompense to all of the Bunces for all the wrongs that had been done to them. On that day would the curse be lifted.'

'And – and has that ever happened?' asked Kate.

'Not yet,' replied Annabel. 'Not yet.'

She sighed and sat down at the table again between the other two. 'And that, Kate, is why I am called Fidelity. A girl Bunce is always given the name in memory of our tragic ancestor and to remind us of when the Bunces were almost the greatest family in the land: and to keep alive the hope that one day the X family will make retribution. I hope that answers your question.'

She bowed her head and a great silence seemed to hang positively in the air.

'Well,' she said after a time, briskly raising her head again. 'We'd better decide about the trifle, hadn't we?'

'Hey,' said Miles, 'you haven't told us the real name of this X family. You said you were going to.'

Annabel sat silent for a while.

'I should never have started this,' she said. 'I didn't mean to.'

'What do you mean, started it? Why not?'

'The real name of the family was Noggins. The rotter, the smooth charmer, was called Albert Noggins.'

Miles' jaw dropped and quivered. 'Gaw!' he said. 'I don't believe you.'

Annabel shrugged, wearily. Clearly, she couldn't care less whether he believed her or not.

'Then who were your ancestors?' she asked, offhandedly but meaningfully.

'I don't know,' said Miles. His face was pale and glistening and he clutched at the corner of the table in order to struggle to his feet. This time, such were the forces that were moving him, he succeeded and he managed to stagger as far as the draining board before collapsing against it.

'You're having me on,' he said. 'You don't really mean it, do you, about the – the –'

'The curse? On you? I'm afraid I do. Course, some people say all the stuff about curses and so on is silly so I shouldn't worry too much. And if you really want to be sure, there's always, well – recompense.'

A car was pulling up outside. Its door was heard to open and close.

'The raspberry trifle,' said Annabel, nodding towards it, 'would be a start.'

Miles nodded eagerly. 'Yeah, yeah,' he said. 'Sure. Take it.'

Annabel reached for the spoon.

The door was pushed open by a larger and older version of Miles. The bulging stomach, cheeks and eyes of his father ought to have served as a constant warning to Miles to mend his ways but so far the example had gone unheeded.

'Oh, no,' said Mr Noggins, glowering at his son, 'not again. Can't you go out anywhere without stuffing yourself full and making yourself sick? Ker-mon.'

He seized Miles by the wrist and started to haul him out.

'Dad, dad,' said Miles, as he was about to disappear through the door, 'is it true that we had an ancestor who was nearly Prime Minister?'

'Gerronoutof it!' said his father, shoving him out of the door.

'But, dad —'

As the door swung to, there was the sound of a blow, followed by a yell. Annabel frowned. She disliked violence. Then she looked down at the raspberry trifle and her face cleared.

'Annabel,' said Kate, 'was that story true? I mean, was any of it true? Even a little bit?'

About to dip the spoon into the trifle, Annabel paused.

'Some things, Kate,' she said, 'are worth fighting for.'

She raised the first spoonful to her lips.

'The Bunces will rise again,' she said.

Savouring it, she gave a happy sigh.

'It is our destiny.'

FRYING AS USUAL
Joan Lingard

Disaster strikes the Francettis when Mr Francetti breaks his leg. Their fish and chip shop never closes, but who is going to run it now that he's in hospital and their mother is in Italy? The answer is quite simple to Toni, Rosita and Paula, and with the help of Grandpa they decide to carry on frying as usual. But it's not that easy . . .

THE FREEDOM MACHINE
Joan Lingard

Mungo dislikes Aunt Janet and to avoid staying with her he decides to hit the open road and look after himself, and with his bike he heads northwards bound for adventure and freedom. But he soon discovers that freedom isn't quite what he'd expected, especially when his food supplies are stolen, and in the course of his journey he learns a few things about himself.

KING DEATH'S GARDEN
Ann Halam

Maurice has discovered a way of visiting the past, and whatever its dangers it's too exciting for him to want to give up – yet. A subtle and intriguing ghost story for older readers.

STRAW FIRE
Angela Hassall

Kevin and Sam meet Mark, an older boy who is sleeping rough up on the Heath behind their street. Kevin feels there is something weird about Mark, something he can't quite put his finger on. And he is soon to discover that there is something very frightening and dangerous about Mark too.

COME BACK SOON
Judy Gardiner

Val's family seem quite an odd bunch and their life is hectic but happy. But then Val's mother walks out on them and Val's carefree life is suddenly quite different. This is a moving but funny story.

COME SING, JIMMY JO
Katherine Paterson

An absorbing story about eleven-year-old Jimmy Jo's rise to stardom, and the problem of coping with fame.

ALL THE WAY TO WITS' END
Sheila Greenwald

Drucilla Brattles has had enough! She's fed up with being surrounded by antiques and heirlooms and she's fed up with wearing ancient dresses. She yearns for a new life: for soft carpets and a cosy home; for decent clothes and for a brace for her teeth, so she'll be able to close her mouth!

Then she hatches a plan, an incredible scheme which turns everyone's lives upside down!

STORM BIRD
Elsie McCutcheon

Torn from her father and her London school, Jenny is sent to live with her grim and sometimes frightening aunt in a small East Anglian seaside town. She is befriended by Josh, son of her aunt's wealthy employers, and shares his secret, passionate interest in birds. But the sinister mystery of her aunt's past begins to haunt Jenny, as it does the whole village. As the web of horror and tragedy is unravelled, Jenny and Josh are thrown together in a gripping climax to this powerful and dramatic story.

SLADE

John Tully

Slade has a mission – to investigate life on Earth. When Eddie discovers the truth about Slade he gets a whole lot more adventure than he bargained for.

WOOF!

Allan Ahlberg

Eric is a perfectly ordinary boy. Perfectly ordinary that is, until the night when, safely tucked up in bed, he slowly but surely turns into a dog! Fritz Wegner's drawings illustrate this funny and exciting story superbly.

THE PRIESTS OF FERRIS

Maurice Gee

Susan Ferris and her cousin Nick return to the world of O which they had saved from the evil Halfmen, only to find that O is now ruled by cruel and ruthless priests. Can they save the inhabitants of O from tyranny? An action-packed and gripping story by the author of prize-winning THE HALFMEN OF O.

THE BEAST MASTER

Andre Norton

Spine-chilling science fiction – treachery and revenge! Hosteen Storm is a man with a mission to find and punish Brad Quade, the man who killed his father long ago on Terra, the planet where life no longer exists.

HALFWAY ACROSS THE GALAXY AND TURN LEFT

Robin Klein

A humorous account of what happens to a family banished from their planet Zygron, when they have to spent a period of exile on Earth.

THE PRIME MINISTER'S BRAIN

Gillian Cross

The fiendish Demon Headmaster plans to gain control of No. 10 Downing Street and lure the Prime Minister into his evil clutches.

RACSO AND THE RATS OF NIMH

Jane Leslie Conly

When fieldmouse Timothy Frisby rescues young Racso, the city rat, from drowning, it's the beginning of a friendship and an adventure. The two are caught up in the struggle of the Rats of NIMH to save their home from destruction. A powerful sequel to MRS FRISBY AND THE RATS OF NIMH.

NICOBOBINUS

Terry Jones

Nicobobinus and his friend, Rosie, find themselves in all sorts of intriguing adventures when they set out to find the Land of the Dragons long ago. Stunningly illustrated by Michael Foreman.